Popular VOTE

Popular VOTE

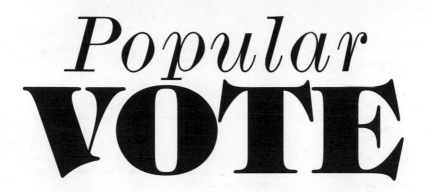

★ ★ ★ ★ ★ ★ ★ ★

MICOL OSTOW

★ ★ ★ ★ ★ ★ ★ ★

★★★★★★★★★ Point ★★★★★★★★★

*To Kate, for coming to NYC and doing her darndest to
keep me sane. And for Yellow. Lots and lots of Yellow.*

Trademarks used herein are owned by their respective trademark owners and
are used without permission.

Library of Congress Cataloging-in-Publication Data

Ostow, Micol.
  Popular vote / Micol Ostow.
    p. cm.
  "Point."
  Summary: In an election year, sixteen-year-old Erin Bright sets aside her
familiar supporting role as daughter of the mayor and girlfriend of the student
body president to stand up for what she believes in and protect an historic park
from being replaced by a gas station.
  ISBN-13: 978-0-545-07521-3
  ISBN-10: 0-545-07521-1
[1. Politics, Practical — Fiction 2. Historic sites — Fiction. 3. High
schools — Fiction. 4. Schools — Fiction. 5. Family life — Illinois — Fiction.
6. Fame — Fiction. 7. Illinois — Fiction.]
I. Title.
  PZ7.O8475Pop 2008
  [Fic] — dc22

                                                        2008004640

SCHOLASTIC, POINT, and associated logos are trademarks and/or registered
trademarks of Scholastic Inc.

Text design by Steve Scott

12 11 10 9 8 7 6 5 4 3 2 1   8 9 10 11 12 13/0

Printed in the U.S.A.
First printing, September 2008

Amongst those who get my enthusiastic vote:

Aimee Friedman, who was kind enough to share her fabulous idea with little old me; Abby McAden, for welcoming me aboard; Jodi Reamer, for swift and sound agenting (with the occasional therapy session thrown in for good measure); the students and faculty at Vermont College, for kicking massive amounts of butt (and especially Uma Krishnaswami, for never letting me get off easy); the Real Lynn Weingarten, for some very necessary company and her mad IM skills; my Mediabistro fall '07 YA writing class, for giving me a reason to change out of my pajamas once a week; and, as always, my family and my Noah. If there were an election for support systems, you all would be top contenders.

They say that familiarity breeds contempt, right? I'm not so sure.

The thing about the familiar is just that: it's a known quantity. It's comforting.

Take this weekend, for example. The girlies and I hit the movies on Saturday night. We caught a romantic comedy starring an anonymous, tanorexic young starlet whose Agent Orange–tinged skin does nothing to deter the love of the bumbling pet-lover who moves into the apartment next door. Obviously, she's allergic to dogs; obviously, they end up together, anyway.

Such is the nature of romantic comedies. And I'm not complaining.

After the movie, we parked ourselves at "our" booth over at Hercules Diner, where we ordered our respective usuals: one order of French toast; one corn muffin, toasted, with grape jelly *on the side* (very key); one cup of decaf coffee, black. Oh, and some cheese fries to split three ways, of course. The waitress didn't even have to write our order down. That's the beauty of the "usual." If it's usual enough, it eventually develops its own momentum.

Plainsboro, Illinois may be a quiet place to grow up, and most of us have known our neighbors since birth. But is that such a bad thing? I say no.

I know we're always being encouraged to pursue the extraordinary, but I think it might just be a matter of adjusting our mind-sets. Maybe it's not "ordinary," but the status quo. In a good way. You know – the party line.

After all, who doesn't love a good party?

Comments (5)

A2Z: So right, girl! And we three do know how 2 par-tay. . . .

brightbabe: it's the truth, speaking of which, can I borrow ur party-tastic pink sequined headband 4 the shoot this week?

Sby16: it's at my house. i'll dig it up.

A2Z: erm, it's possible that I wore it to the football game last week and *maybe* it slipped off and disappeared. Maybe. But maybe it's still there. i think it's still there. i mean, i *know*! it's there. i'll find it. 4 sher, shelby.

brightbabe: seriously, girlz. Pink sequins are rad, but maybe not worth getting so worked up about? Just a suggestion (heresy, I know). I'm sure we can come up with a plan B. See u both tomorrow! XX

✫ Chapter One

Things people know about me, Erin Bright:

1) I keep a diligent blog detailing the delicious trivialities of being a junior at Plainsboro High School in Plainsboro, Illinois.

2) Lavender is my signature color, and cashmere is my fave fabric.

3) My father is the mayor of Plainsboro.

4) My boyfriend is Logan Tanner.

Things people do not know about me:

1) The second toe on both of my feet is slightly longer than my big toe, which is gross. Open-toed shoes are not my friends.

2) As much as I love Plainsboro, I've been here my whole life and sometimes it feels a teensy bit, well . . . teensy.

3) In addition to my blog, I keep a journal. Yes, a journal. The old-fashioned kind that you use

with a pen. I write in it almost every day, before school, from my perch on the wooden bench tucked into a corner of Everett Field. What I write in it is a lot different than my blog. And no, you can't read it.

That should be enough information to get us started, don't you think?

☆ ☆ ☆ ☆ ☆

"It's like you said on your blog, Erin — people totally fear change."

My best friend Shelby says this decisively, like it's something that she's been turning over in her brain for a good forty-two minutes. Which, seeing as how we just got finished with trig class, she probably has.

My other best friend, Zoë, snickers from her seat on the opposite side of our lunch table. "That must explain why Mrs. Moore wears the same outfit every single day."

Zoë doesn't like trig, either, but in her case, her resentment seems mainly focused on our stylistically challenged educator.

"You don't know that," I point out. I fish a carton of low-fat yogurt out of my eco-friendly canvas lunch bag and peel its lid off slowly to avoid artificially flavored cherry backsplash on my brand-new, short-sleeved, lilac cashmere sweater. Dad has a photo shoot later today and he needs Mom and me looking flawless.

"Maybe she has five identical versions of the exact same outfit," I say, then gulp down a spoonful of yogurt.

Zoë rolls her eyes. "That would be weird."

"She's a *math* teacher," I remind her. "She chose to devote her life to math. She is clearly no stranger to weirdness." But honestly? Mrs. Moore's crimes of fashion are victimless. Maybe we should cut her a break.

Shelby smiles, freckles exploding across her alabaster skin. "And what's your GPA in trig this semester, Erin?" she teases.

"The semester just started," I demur, stirring my spoon inside my yogurt cup. "So, you know — maybe it's just that I fear change."

Shelby shakes her head good-naturedly. "So that's why we're always sitting at our regular lunch table." She slaps her manicured hand palm-down against the sticky plastic tabletop, then wrinkles her nose when she notices the stick. "Which maybe they could sponge off every now and then."

"Erin?"

6

I look up from my lunch to see Logan pursing his lips at me in mild frustration. He's flanked on either side by Theo and Paige, as usual. Theo is Logan's running mate, and Paige basically helps them to manage their campaign. Speaking of things that stay the same . . .

"Weren't we going to meet by your locker after last period ended?" my boyfriend asks pointedly. "To talk campaign strategy?"

Busted. But his eyes are twinkling so I can tell he's not really mad.

It's hard to get Logan really mad. To be honest, I think I've only ever seen him at a personal beige alert, or maybe, under extreme circumstances, a buttery yellow. All in all, Logan Tanner is a very down-to-earth kind of guy. This is what makes him:

1) an earnest-yet-unwavering advocate on behalf of the Plainsboro High School student body
and
2) a super-extra-adorable and delicious boyfriend

I sit up straight in my plastic lunchroom seat, fearlessly ignoring the practical joke that static electricity is playing on my hair-straightening balm. I assume my "serious" expression, which involves pushing my Diet Snapple pink lemonade aside. (I realize Diet Snapple is not an especially serious beverage.)

Logan practically *is* the status quo (in the good way, I mean. Of course). We're starting our third year as boyfriend and girlfriend — his senior year, my junior. It's also his third consecutive year running as PHS student body president (freshmen aren't allowed to run or he probably would have swept those ballots as well).

People like Logan as president. You could almost call it destiny. Something about his broad shoulders and wanton use of fifty-cent vocab words make him a ringer, make people feel safe. Really, these yearly lunchtime brainstorming sessions we have are pretty much a joke at this point. Boy's a shoe-in.

"I need a catchy slogan," he insists. Zoë slides to the left to make room for Logan at the table. Paige and Theo crouch. "For the posters and stuff."

Shelby, Zoë, and I exchange amused glances. He's so cute when he's irrationally insecure. "You're running uncontested," I point out.

"As usual," Shelby whispers, just loudly enough so that I can hear her.

Logan frowns. *Of course* he is running uncontested.

He has run uncontested ever since sophomore year, when groundswell support was so . . . *swollen* that the only other candidate, Missy Jackson (a dark horse by anyone's standards, poor thing), dropped out at the eleventh hour (aka third period of student government election day). It would have been a scandal, except for how fervently I was gunning for Team Logan. Missy eventually joined the social action committee, and all was well in the world of PHS. And has been ever since.

"Don't you see, though?" Logan says, touching my arm (it still gives me shivers). "That's just it."

I'm not sure *what's* just it, exactly, so I just nod. "Mmmm."

"I can't let my history in student government make me complacent."

What did I tell you about the vocab words? It should surprise no one that we first met as cotutors in the peer-to-peer English mentoring program.

But he's coming to me in all earnestness, as he does every year, and, as earnestness involves *major* display of his insanely adorable left-cheek dimple, I do my best to concentrate.

Suddenly, inspiration hits. I lean forward. "Logan for Prez: Out-*TAN*-ding!" I waggle my fingers in a little "jazz hands" gesture for extra flair.

He sighs. "Uh . . ."

9

"People like a good pun," Shelby jumps in helpfully.

I shoot her a grateful grin. People *do* like a good pun. Me-people especially, that is. But I feel confident that I can speak for the common student.

Logan chews on his full lower lip. "Yeah, I think that puns may be, like, the lowest common denominator for humor."

"That's the point." I cough delicately. "That's what my dad always says, anyway."

Logan brightens. "Really? Your dad?"

I can tell he's already rethinking the value of the lowest common denominator. My father, he of the photo shoots, press conferences, and impeccable presentation, has that effect on people.

Now it's my turn to sigh. "Yup. Caleb Bright thinks that judicious use of humor demonstrates warmth," I offer. And Caleb Bright knows from warmth.

Caleb Bright — my father — is the mayor of Plainsboro. Has been, in fact, for the last four years. Which means — yep, you guessed it — that this is an election year.

I, Erin Bright, am not only First Girlfriend of Plainsboro High but I'm the town's First Daughter, too.

It's a lot of pressure.

Of course, Dad's always been high-profile, ever since I was little, when he was a razzle-dazzle lawyer advocating on behalf of the state. After racking up a bajillion community service awards and winning a record-breaking gazillion cases for the government (estimated figures), it was barely a leap over to politics proper. More like a sidle. And Caleb Bright is deft with the fancy footwork (seriously — you should see him at the annual county dinner dance). So my mom and I have been prepped for the small-town limelight from way back when. Appearances matter. Hence my extreme caution with regard to such hazards as rogue yogurt cartons.

But as my dad is quick to point out, appearances aren't *all* that matter. You can be cute as a button or brimming with steely confidence, and if you don't have the goods to back that up, you're toast.

Dad's got the goods. He is calm and commanding, but respectful in a way that never comes across as condescending. High-powered corporate people, young mothers with wobbly toddlers, high school kids who really can't be bothered to care much about anything — they all love my father. It's this X-factor, this chemistry thing. He just has It.

Logan has It, too. Or, if he's too young for full-on It-age, at least he has an It-let. But every now and

11

then he has these moments of self-doubt. Like, once a year. That's when he hunkers down with Zoë, Shelby, Theo, Paige, and me to talk campaign strategy, slogans, posters, giveaways. And it's up to us to remind him that he has It in the bag.

Of course, that's easier said than done. Especially because, as you see, Logan and I don't always see eye to eye on his platform.

"I guess I just worry that being too jokey detracts from my credibility," he says, drumming his fingers on the table thoughtfully.

"Okay, nobody's asking you to ad-lib your favorite Dane Cook riff during the debate," I clarify. "But I think if you can laugh at yourself, it makes you a little more . . . human." As opposed to gorgeously perfect and godlike, which he is. It's a little ridiculous.

"I don't know." He shakes his head.

"All right, admit it. You hate my suggestion." I laugh. "You're going to go all serious, all the time. You're actually going to stomp through the halls glaring at everyone between now and election day." I make a *grr*-y, glarey sort of face. "And your public will love you for your gravitas."

"Your face is going to freeze that way, babe," he says, grinning. I know he loves our sparring and our differing points of view just as much as I do. In the end, like I said, he'll go with his own decision. Which is fine — it got him this far, didn't it? His job is to be PHS president. My job is to be the president's girlfriend.

I can do that. Really well, actually.

He reaches out to brush a strand of hair out of my eyes and I duck. "Almost as bad as my face freezing in a scowl would be for you to make my hair all screwy," I say, shoving his hands away, making it all playful. "Dad's got a pre-election photo shoot this afternoon, and I swore I'd come home straight from school, picture-perfect." The Plainsboro populace needs to see its royal family on pristine display in its natural habitat. Not that I'm complaining — photo shoots mean fun with lip gloss.

Logan holds his hands up in an "uncle" gesture. He totally gets it. Among the various things in my life that must stay the same? That absolutely cannot change? My flat-ironed hair. My spotless sweater. And the popularity ratings of both of the guys in my life.

☆ Chapter Two

"Smile pretty, people! And say . . ."

"Victory!" I offer, flashing my pearly whites. I earned them after three long years spent suffering in braces.

"Perfect!" Ted, the photographer, disappears behind the camera.

Then he sighs, placing his hands on his hips and looking around our living room. "We need something stately . . . something mayoral . . . something . . . different," he muses. He's not feeling our shoot, the stiff, portraity poses.

"What if we all posed in our bathing suits?" I suggest. "Or Dad could be lying across the couch and Mom and I could be behind him, leaning over, you know, like game show host assistants." I do my jazz hands again. They're so all-purpose.

Obviously I'm kidding. To lighten the mood, you

14

see. Ted's been Dad's official photographer since his first campaign, and while we adore him and trust him to catch us at our most attractive, most intelligent-looking, and most persuasive, the truth is . . . well, after all this time, there really isn't much different that we can do. It's kind of all been covered.

"Bathing suits. Very dignified." My mother pretends to be impatient with me, but I can tell that her eyes are smiling, even if her mouth isn't. It'd be different if she thought I was serious, but come on. Me? A liability? During *campaign season*?

Unlikely.

"If you've got it, Mom, flaunt it. Who knows? You may only have a few good years left." As if. My mother's abs are ten times flatter than my own. She is the Pilates queen. I keep hoping that some of that muscle tone is genetic — if latent — but so far, I mostly take after my tall, lanky father.

"I'm going to pretend you didn't say that," my mother says, turning to my father and dusting some invisible lint off his shoulder. "Different, Caleb?" she asks. "Any ideas? Ideas that don't involve partial nudity, that is?"

"You're no fun," I grumble.

"Fun!" my father says, a glint in his wide, expressive eyes. "That's it."

15

"Rollerblades?" I ask hopefully. How much would I rock a seventies-style flip and mod makeup in a Roller Derby–themed photo shoot?

"Maybe slightly less fun than that," my father amends. "But they've seen me in office. They've seen me at rallies, debates, and town hall meetings. Maybe the key this time around is to lighten up, show them that I'm really just an average Joe."

Average Joe. Ha. My father is anything but average. Still, he may be on to something.

"What are you thinking, Mayor?" Ted asks. Ted's so sweet, the way he's still all formal and polite with my dad after all this time.

"Maybe a spread of the three of us doing something domestic," Dad says, clearly thinking out loud. "Cooking? Making breakfast?"

"Breakfast says 'cozy' and 'homey,'" my mother puts in, warming to the idea. "The voters of Plainsboro would love to have breakfast with Caleb Bright."

"And pajamas are comfy without being *too* undignified," I add. Fuzzy slippers and matchy flannel pj sets are cute. I can live with that wardrobe choice, especially since, with hair and makeup on hand to keep us primped, there's no danger of bed-head or pillow-creased cheeks.

16

"Breakfast is fun," Ted confirms. Relief settles across his face and deep into his startlingly sharp cheekbones. Sometimes I think Ted is hanging out on the wrong side of the lens. "Do you have a cappuccino machine?"

"We do," my mother says, running her manicured fingers through her stick-straight blond hair. "But" — her green eyes glint — "better than that is our waffle iron."

Ted nods and does a little "not worthy" half-genuflect gesture. "Perfecto."

The First Family does waffles. I love it. I'm spraying twelve pounds of Reddi-wip on mine.

My father heads off to the kitchen with Ted to discuss lighting and blocking and stuff while my mother whirls into action.

"I'm going to pick a few sets of pajamas and robes and bring them to Mena for final approval. Nothing sexy, but nothing frumpy, either. She'll know what works. You —" She grabs me by the shoulders and physically rotates me so I'm turned away from her and toward the dining room, where Ted's team has set up base camp. "Get Frannie to retouch your makeup. No one wakes up in the morning in pink pearlescent Bonne Belle. Tell her you need a natural look. Matte shadow. No liner."

17

Mena and Frannie are hair and makeup, respectively. If anyone can help my mother, father, and me all wear the ell-hay out of our sensible sleepwear, it's Mena and Frannie.

It feels like only moments later that we're all three coiffed, painted, and posed in the kitchen, me demurely cross-legged on the imported-marble countertop, balancing the aforementioned tower of whipped-cream-garnished blueberry waffles (the ratio of Reddi-wip to waffle is something like 3:1). Mom and Dad stand side by side, pillars of the Plainsboro community, a new, decidedly yummier twist on the whole American Gothic aesthetic. They each brandish a gargantuan cup of coffee that doesn't even come close to representing the amount of caffeine they both ingest each day. Dad managed to scrounge up some cornflower-blue pinstriped pajamas, over which he's belted a smoking jacket just so. Because he is Caleb Bright, of course, the smoking jacket takes on a very "British academic" vibe that perfectly offsets the playful tone of the shoot.

The campaign season has just kicked off, and the Brights are already killing it.

Ted fiddles with another button on the side of his camera, steps back, then steps forward and peers through the lens again. "Take two, lovelies," he says. "Smile and say 'victory.'"

The word rolls right off our tongues.

☆ ☆ ☆ ☆ ☆

The next morning, I'm sipping at a nonfat latte, legs swinging over my favorite park bench. My journal is in my lap as I savor the quiet of the early morning, when a shadow falls over the blank page of my open journal. I look up to see Logan. He looks . . . tense.

"Hey." I smile, scooting down and patting the bench next to me so that he knows to sit. The air smells crisp, like fall, and while I value my alone time at Everett Field, I value my Logan time, too.

Once he's settled, I give him a quick kiss. Nothing too extreme since we're dangerously close to school property, but still. He's Logan. What could be a better way to start my morning?

"I knew I'd find you here," he says, "writing." He ruffles my hair lightly.

"Just call me Edwina," I say.

Logan is the only person in my life with whom I've shared my dirty little secret. There's one thing in this world that I'm more passionate about than lavender

19

cashmere, and that's Edwina St. Claire. She was an English teacher at PHS once upon a time, until she decided to devote herself to her own writing. She's a famous, late author from Plainsboro who did her best writing from Everett Field, back when it was expansive and vast. Now it's a thick, grassy field just behind our high school — and one of my fave places to hang, alone with my thoughts. I do my best writing on the park bench that's been set up to memorialize her.

Anyway, Edwina's the reason I write anything at all, even if I'm not so sure that my blog is exactly what she had in mind when she encouraged young women everywhere to "write their hearts."

"Edwina," he says affectionately. Then his soft blue eyes turn serious. "Erin."

"Oh, no," I start. "You seem way too purposeful." I hate to get all purposeful this early in the morning, especially when things were taking a turn for the romantic.

"I wanted to tell you last night, but you were all cheerful and excited about the photo shoot," he admits. Now he looks wistful. This can't be good.

"Tell me what?" My suspicions are way up.

"Keep in mind I am only reporting what I know," he says, dragging things out so that I want to scream.

"But the school board announced last night that —"
He looks away, then back, as if he's forcing himself
to look straight into my eyes. "They're selling Everett
Field."

"*What?*" My heart flutters in my chest. Why would
they do this? "Who are they selling it to?"

Logan shrugs. "It's a company called the Caswell
Corporation. I don't know much about them."

My mind races. Maybe it's not as bad as it sounds.
Maybe the folks at Caswell don't plan to actually do
anything with the field. Why do I care so much,
anyway?

Maybe it will still be there for me every morning,
for my routine of lattes and letters.

Judging from the look on Logan's face, though?
Yeah, that's not happening. And I do care, more than
I'd ever have thought I would about something not-
Logan, and even, really, not-me.

"Why is the school board selling?" I ask. "They've
always been so proud of the field and how it's a historic
site and all that."

"They want to raise cash for a private arts
program."

"But it's a *public school*," I say, snappish.

"A public school that will attract lots of attention

from colleges if it can boast a fancy-schmancy arts program," Logan says, sounding altogether too logical for my liking. He wraps a comforting hand around my own.

The truth is, I can get behind something like the arts. Edwina St. Claire would have been way into an arts program. So maybe this is all in keeping with the spirit of my personal heroine. Maybe. I allow myself another glimmer of hope, and a beat or two to breathe.

"What are they going to do with the field?" I ask finally.

It's Logan's hesitation that tells me I'm really not going to like the answer.

He hedges, jiggling his leg against the bench. I press my hand over his knee, forcing him still.

He leans forward and kisses me on the forehead. This is so not going to be good.

"They're putting up . . . a gas station," he admits finally.

My mouth drops open in an "O" of utter disbelief.

For a moment Logan wisely says nothing. What can there be for him to say? What could possibly take the sting away from this news?

"I . . . think they'll sell coffee there," he manages at

last. "So you can still get your morning fix?" He's trying to make a joke. It's . . . not funny.

Logan squeezes my hand. For the first time ever in our fabulous and oh-so-politically successful relationship, it doesn't help.

Debate always rages about whether or not the personal should be made political. Or at least, that's what Ms. Donatello, aka Awesomest Social Studies Teacher EVER, is constantly telling me. I think she worries about my role models. She frets that my mother's not Hillary enough to my father's Bill. That I'm not Chelsea.

'Cause I'm not. Really, I'm not. Don't get me wrong, I *care,* and I'm so totally proud of everything my dad's done for Plainsboro (did you know that ever since he set up a neighborhood watch, local retailers have reported a thirty-two percent drop in theft?), but when it comes to my own personal platform, well, it turns out that . . . really, it's just personal.

Take the whole Everett Field thing. I've got some reliable intel on this entire sordid state of affairs. Logan Tanner (class prez and *mi amore,* of course) informs me that PHS is planning on selling the field to the Caswell Corporation (boo, hiss!) in order to raise the cash for a new arts program. And while I'm all for the arts, Caswell is planning to pave over the field and turn it into a gas station. A *gas station.*

Now, yes, an arts program will be mucho helpful if our school district is going to stay competitive (and, more important, if we plan to *learn*).

But does learning and keeping ahead really have to come at the expense of a beautiful historic landmark like Everett Field? It was, indeed, the site of my very first date with Logan (he surprised me with a picnic . . . swoon), but I can't be the only one with sentimental attachments to that patch of grass. Do progress and payoff have to equal *trade-off*?

I don't think so. Razing Everett Field for *any* cause – noble or no – is not a step forward. It's a step back.

Change is inevitable, sure. But that doesn't mean I have to like it. Or even take it lying down.

Comments (2)

princelogan: I'm on your side as always, babe. But this might sound more convincing from someone who wasn't wearing her pajamas. ;)

A2Z: he's right. Especially since they're probably lavender cashmere.

Logan and Zoë had my number, obvs. But for once I wasn't sure that I wanted them to. For once I wanted to be left alone to ride off into the sunset on my high horse. It was an unfamiliar feeling for me. I wasn't sure what to do about it. I sat up in bed and smoothed down my pajamas — a lavender cashmere tank and shorts set, of course — and scanned the reading material piled high on my nightstand. Edwina's masterpiece was on top. I couldn't go the *Restless Nature* route tonight — it hit too close to home.

Tonight was going to be totally *In Touch,* all the way. For old time's sake.

☆ Chapter Three

"It —" *huff* — "looks so peaceful from here." *Huff.* "Almost like it has no idea what's in store for it."

"First of all, Erin, it's a *field*. A very pretty field, sure, but at the end of the day? More of a strip of flora. Not a sad, pathetic creature to be pitied."

"That's where you're wrong, my friend. It's the flora that needs our help. What with being inanimate and all. Did you learn nothing from *The Lorax*?" *Huff.* "And besides, that was only one thing. You had no second of all."

"The second of all was that if you keep trying to make grand political statements while we run laps, you're going to give yourself a coronary. Or zits. From the stress."

Touché. I slow my pace a beat or two and take some deep, cleansing breaths. *Huuuuuffff.*

I am trying to get Shelby and Zoë to see my point of view, but it isn't working all that well. For her part, Zoë is slightly concerned, but it seems mostly to have to do with my excessive perspiration. I guess that's why, of the two, Shelby is the one I'm more likely to bare my soul to. When I'm in a soul-baring mood, that is.

My first mistake may have been to address this issue during gym class. Nobody is at their freshest while running laps in the forty-two-degree morning chill, even if we do have a nice view of the very field that has sparked my internal *Sturm und Drang*.

"I'm sorry if I'm getting a little spazzy," I say, trying to sound less like a left-wing lunatic and more like a reasonable member of mainstream society, "but it's Everett Field. It's the most romantic place in Plainsboro."

Zoë snorts. "Clearly Logan has never taken you to Le Petite Auberge for dinner."

We've actually been to that restaurant three times, for birthdays mostly. It's really pretty, and everything is French and rich and dripping with butter, which, *yum*. But that's so not the point right now.

"Don't go into the blah-blah picnic story," Zoë begs, before I can interject. "We know the blah-blah picnic story. We've heard the story. We could probably each recite it from memory, if we had to." She rolls her brown eyes daintily, as only she can do.

"Edwina St. Claire wrote *Restless Nature* from the field gazebo!" I sputter. "Edwina St. Claire. The greatest female essayist of all time." And as much as I truly detest running laps, being out here in the fresh air, inhaling the scent of fresh-cut grass . . . I feel like I might have some sense of what she was on about.

As we've discussed, I am very into Edwina St. Claire. Shelby and Zoë can be forgiven for not knowing quite how much, as I haven't really told anyone about this, but it's my secret dream to someday be a writer like she was. Except without the living in a tent for four years and the premature death and all that. I think a talented writer can live in an actual house with indoor plumbing and turn out a perfectly good piece of work — with the right amount of discipline and coffee (and nail polish!), that is.

But anyway. Logan is the only one who knows how much Edwina St. Claire means to me, and even he doesn't know the whole story. Because she is a homegrown heroine, our English department is extremely keen on working her into our curriculum. Unfortunately, her *Walden*-meets-e. e. cummings-esque ramblings aren't exactly the most accessible. That's why I am constantly finding myself reviewing *Restless Nature* as a peer-to-peer tutor with some terrified freshman who doesn't know the first thing about water metaphors, the symbolism of trees, and the various poetic interpretations of the color green.

Logan understood about the color green. And after a month or so of not-so-subtly listening in on my tutoring sessions (our desks were arranged perpendicularly, so it's not like he had a choice. It was a good setup for my love life, less so for the whole learning process), he knew that the way to win me over was via Edwina St. Claire and, ergo, via Everett Field. Picnic, smooching, and other miscellaneous lovey-doveyness ensued shortly.

Le Petite Auberge has *nothing* on Everett Field, in my opinion.

"I just can't believe that Logan isn't more worked up about this," I say, jogging along reluctantly. It is my personal belief that running laps is an insidious and slow-acting form of torture (see above re: laps, detestation of). "It's his memory, too."

"Exactly," Shelby says, not even remotely winded. Her cheeks are flushed and her eyes twinkle. She looks like a pixie doll. Mind you, Z and I are both well aware that there is nothing babydoll-esque about her personality. More like a bulldog. Or a firecracker.

Shelby is the most athletic of the three of us. She does an hour on her parents' elliptical machine every morning before school. She says it clears her head. Sheer insanity.

"*Memory,*" she goes on. "Singular. As in, one of many that the two of you share. And therefore, probably not worth getting his boxer-briefs in a bunch."

"Excuse you. Considering that I have no firsthand knowledge of Logan's preference in undergarments, I think it best if we leave them out of the conversation." A lady never tells, after all.

Zoë smirks. I can tell she thinks I have completely lost my mind. Maybe she's right. "Whatever. What is it that you want him to do, anyway? Chain himself to the gazebo wearing a sandwich board?"

I shrug, as much as one can shrug while pretending to jog. "There has to be something. Everyone at PHS loves him. He has clout."

"Not with the school board," Shelby points out. "They're the ones who would have to approve or disapprove the sale. Student council has nothing to do with that."

"Fine, okay," I say, waving my hand at her. "Technically speaking, you're right. But if he started a petition, the school board would have to pay attention.

And maybe he could raise money for the arts program. How much could an arts program possibly cost? Then we wouldn't need to sell the field."

"Those are possibilities," Shelby admits, "but long shots. I think an arts program might actually be kind of expensive." One eyebrow shoots up delicately. "State-of-the-art media is not cheap."

"Thanks," I grumble.

"That's what friends are for, Er," Shelby insists. "To give you the cold, hard truth when you need it. You know I'm on your side, but it's an uphill battle. It might not be worth it for Logan to risk getting the school board all hot and bothered."

She has a point, which I grudgingly acknowledge with uncharacteristic silence.

"If I were you, I'd grab a blade of grass from the field and a sliver of wood from the gazebo, and press the heck out of them in my scrapbook," she advises. "But then?"

I look at her. "Yeah?"

"I'd stand by your man." She clearly means for this to be the end of our conversation.

Country music logic. Agh. How can I argue?

☆ ☆ ☆ ☆ ☆

Even after a (semi-)brisk run to burn off some of my righteous indignation, I'm still riled up by the time fifth period rolls around. It's a good thing I've got social studies with Ms. Donatello, a redheaded hummingbird of a teacherly type. If she had lived in the twenties, she totally would have been a flapper. Or a suffragette. Both, actually. That was kind of the point of the twenties, wasn't it?

I'm losing my focus, if not my mind. Dashed romantic dreams mixed up with first-period phys ed will do that to a girl. Even if the girl is typically unflappable. Yeah, I'm flapping.

Fortunately, Ms. Donatello has it together, right down to the tips of her black plastic glasses frames. She's like the love child of Lisa Loeb and Elvis Costello. I allow myself to wonder briefly how my father would react if I were to come home one day with a cherry-red, blunt-banged bob and a wardrobe straight out of the Salvation Army.

Ha. It's good for a smile.

"You seem worked up about something today, Erin," Ms. Donatello observes as I collapse at my desk. The person who occupied it just before me was kind enough to leave a wad of chewed-up gum stuck on its underside. Lovely.

I'm not too surprised that she can tell, even though I've toned down my snit over the last period or so. Ms. D is intuitive that way. Hence her being my favorite teacher. She's also the student council advisor.

I bite my lip. "You know..." Complaining to my friends is one thing, but Ms. D. is a teacher, albeit an especially cool teacher.

She raises an eyebrow at me, but doesn't push it.

The rest of the class files in. Papers rustle, pen caps click open, cell phones are stashed away in book bags. We are sponges.

Ms. D. stands at the front of the room, hands on her hips. "Today we're going to talk about the democratic process," she says.

"Like checks and balances?" someone chimes in from behind me.

Ms. D. says, "I was hoping to go a little bit deeper than that." This is so Ms. D. Once we've blasted through the textbook stuff, she likes to rouse us in a conversation of actual relevant current events. Normally, I lap that stuff up. Today ... ? Meh.

"I'd like to hear your thoughts about times throughout history — or now, of course — when the democratic process has failed our country."

"Like the chads and Florida." It's Theo Walker,

also known as Logan's best friend and constant running mate. Theo's the type of guy who gets along with everybody.

"Chads" refer to the first G.W. Bush election, where he lost the popular vote but still won the presidency. Some people are still kind of bent out of shape about that.

"That would be a good example," Ms. D. agrees, nodding so that the edges of her hair swish back and forth against her chin.

"That's a *terrible* example." Leave it Allie Soren, a pinched-face blond with a pointy chin and hair like a home perm, to kill the class buzz. Not to be unnecessarily nasty, but it's true. She has the personality to match her wiry, edgy, nervous looks.

"Yes, Allie?" Ms. D. asks with patient bemusement.

"Well, the whole point of our election system is that it reflects the political climate. And whatever." She folds her arms primly across the top of her desk.

"It's called the popular vote," Theo mutters, just loudly enough to get a snicker from some other kids. "Look it up."

"This is what's known as a lively debate," Ms. D. says, smirking with satisfaction. "Keep it up, guys."

"The real problem is when the popular vote has no venue for expression," I say, half to myself. Realizing

I've spoken out loud, I straighten in my seat and raise my hand.

"Erin?" Ms. D. says.

I didn't exactly mean to speak out of turn, and I don't have my thoughts all that well organized, both of which are unusual for me. "Uh," I stammer, "well . . . for instance . . . if, you know, a historical site was threatened." There. "And it was something that was useful for sustainability." Ms. D. loves any mention of "sustainability." I carry on, warming up. "But it's controlled by government, not by the public."

"Isn't it the public that elects the government?" Allie asks.

"That doesn't mean that government always acts completely within our interests," I shoot back, my cheeks now flaming the color of Ms. Donatello's hair. I'm not sure how my father would feel about this mini-rant of mine. I'm starting to sweat again. Obviously there's just not enough Lady Speed Stick in the world.

"It's a process. It isn't ideal," Theo says, stepping in gracefully.

I nod, grateful. "I agree. I'm just saying."

I think I'm saying . . . that the whole situation with Everett Field has me feeling even lousier than I realized.

But — as much as it pains me to agree with Allie

Soren — it's just part of the democratic process. And like Theo says, the process isn't ideal.

In other words, it's icky, but there isn't a whole lot for *me* to do about it.

Unfortunately.

☆ ☆ ☆ ☆ ☆

My mother's First Lady shtick does not extend to Martha Stewart—esque multicourse sit-down dinners. The truth is, most nights my dad's off at big meetings where he has to wear suits with matching ties and dress socks, and Mom and I are left to our own devices, scrambling up egg-white omelets and eating in front of the evening news. Which is what we're doing right now. Tonight is goat cheese and mushroom, my favorite. I inhale deeply and soak up the aroma. It's not quite the same as a "home-cooked" meal, but the eggs were home-cracked, anyway. And the smooth leather of our sectional sofa feels cool against the skin of my shorts-clad legs.

An anchorwoman with regrettably layered hair shrieks about the latest celebutante to be hospitalized for "exhaustion." Sarcasm drips from the corners of her emerald-lined eyelids. I'm kind of sleepy myself.

"Exhaustion." My mother sighs, echoing my

thoughts, and smiles at me. "Who knew that was a clinical diagnosis?"

Please. As if the pressures of perfection would ever take their toll on Mom. I want to inform her that actually, I'm the one who's cracking. The First Daughter is losing her marbles. And over a scraggly patch of grass that, until yesterday, I wouldn't have thought meant any more to me than my grass-green sheepskin-lined Ugg boots.

I mean, if I'm going to be a writer, I'm going to be a writer, field or no field. Right?

"Obviously these starlets aren't getting their calcium," I quip, stabbing at a stray hunk of goat cheese that peeks from the folds of my omelet. It's easier to focus on infotainment than on my own systematic breakdown.

"Who knows?" my mother muses. "They live in a bubble. They lose sight of their priorities."

I know from bubbles. I mean, just a couple of days ago I was photographed in my cotton pj capris, eating breakfast. At night. With flawless, flat-ironed hair and airbrushed skin.

Have I lost sight of what's real?

I do a quick mental inventory. Family: check. My parents rock. I love them and do lots to prove it, including allowing said pictures of myself in sleepwear to be published for the viewing public. That's big. I mean, how many girls would even consider leaving the house in their nighties? Much less committing the image to film?

I didn't think so.

Friends: check. Shelby and Zoë know I have their backs, and vice versa. What are friends for, if not to warn you about the dangerous effects of leggings under miniskirts (they don't work, even with beanpole legs like mine. *Trust me*)? Shelby is all fire and honesty, aggressive as her hair is red, and funny, too. Zoë has naturally ink-black hair, and a little less heart, maybe, but she's wicked funny, and someone who you always want around. We're like Charlie's Angels, but with cuter clothes. And without the violence.

(Does that make me Cameron Diaz? That would be nice. Hmm . . .)

Romance: check. I heart Logan. That's why, at tomorrow's student council pre-election debate, I'm going to sit in the very first row and lob him a few soft-ball questions that the two of us have carefully planned out in advance. ("What's your position on themed proms?" "Can we bring Smart Water to the lunch-room vending machines?" "After-school art electives: college-transcript boosters or shameless ploys for extra credit?")

I am definitely *not* going to ask his position on the sale of Everett Field. I mean, I already know his position. Don't I?

But isn't there another way to raise the arts program money without giving up a historic landmark? Isn't there a way to get the school board to take our voice into account? There *has* to be.

But I'm not going to be the one to bring it up. Not to Logan, not in front of the entire student body, and not tomorrow. Not me.

I've got my priorities in order, after all.

Even though (and this is just between you and me) — sometimes? Priorities stink.

http://firstgirlbright.blogorama.com

September 21, 5:18 pm

Today was supposed to go so much differently.

<u>Comments (0)</u>

☆ *Chapter Four*

To say that I put my foot in my mouth this afternoon at the student council debate would be a vast understatement. Sort of like calling Britney Spears's parenting style "mildly erratic."

I'm a good student. Above-average grades without dipping into genius/savant/social-pariah territory. I'm popular but friendly and (I think) well liked. I always invite the whole grade to my birthday parties, even though that involves enough frosting to feed an army of Girl Scouts for a year. Normal-pretty, if prone to breakouts when I've gotten a little too chummy with the chocolate fudge brownie frozen yogurt. Supportive. Worthy of the title of Girlfriend to the Presumed President-Elect.

I've *been* all of these things. Up until now.

Now things are different. Erratic. *Majorly* erratic.

As of 2:48 P.M., I'm no longer the Worthy Girlfriend to the Presumed President-Elect.

Now I am officially a Girlfriend Non Grata.

Officially. Like, they should make me a plaque the way they made one for my dad when they gave him the key to the city.

Here's how it all went down.

☆ ☆ ☆ ☆ ☆

"Is my tie straight?"

Logan smelled of orange Tic Tacs and Paul Mitchell Freeze and Shine Hairspray, both of which were courtesy of me. I had the whole pre-debate routine down to a science.

I patted his chest, taking a split second to savor the contact, even if it was of the PG-13 variety. Unable to resist his clean, earnest — and yes, adorably nervous — expression, I leaned forward and planted a quick kiss on his lips. "Your tie is perfect." I grabbed at his hand and squeezed it in my own. "I have to sit. Go kick butt!"

He winked at me, and I disappeared from behind the wings to find my place among the rest of the plebes.

(I know the drill. Heck, I practically run the drill, now that I've been through two of these with Logan already.)

The gym smelled like aged sweat and ammonia, a heady combination that made me dizzy. I smacked discreetly on a piece of Dentyne Ice in the hopes of instituting sensory overload. Even though I knew Logan had it in the bag, I still felt a fluttery little sensation just at the base of my throat. Not butterflies, exactly, but possibly Mexican jumping beans that were halfway cooked.

Theo, Shelby, Zoë, and I positioned ourselves in the first row. Usually Shelby prefers to situate herself more centrally, all the better to keep an eye on whether or not her latest crush, Tripp Roberts, is keeping an eye on *her*, but in this case, she made an exception. The greater good and all. It's a running theme.

Logan's not actually running *against* anyone this semester, which is part of why it's hard to take his low-grade panic all that seriously. Okay, technically, one too many students could abstain from the vote and Logan would be left out in the dust. But that's so not going to happen.

So really, this "debate" is less of a point-counterpoint thing, and more of a Q&A. Friendly.

Innocent. No one's ever all that concerned about muckraking, rabble-rousing, or gossip-mongering rearing its head at one of these things.

No one would ever have expected that the Rabble McMucky-Monger, aka the Worst Girlfriend in the World, would be *me*.

Ms. Donatello took the podium and introduced the candidate. As if Logan needed any introduction. We've talked about his dimples, right?

I donned my "thoughtful" glasses (I'm nearsighted, but usually wear contacts unless I'm in the mood to look smarter) and leaned forward in my seat. Zoë thumbed at her cell phone. For all I know, she was texting me, but my concentration was on Logan. Those Mexican jumping beans were acting up again. Shelby twisted in her seat, pretending to look at the clock on the wall behind us but really looking at Tripp, who was, thankfully, making freaky-smitten eyes right back at her. Theo flipped idly through some note cards in his hands, which I thought was a particularly cute touch, since it was Logan who was actually, you know, up there *speaking*.

Paige Wilkins asked the first question. As we've discussed, Paige is good friends with both Theo and Logan, and she can usually be heard pushing the liberal ticket in our social studies class. It isn't unusual for her to ask a question during a debate. I just hoped she would leave the Smart Water thing alone — that one was all mine.

Ms. D. scooted down off of the auditorium stage and over to where Paige stood in the audience, passing the microphone down the aisle toward Paige with an encouraging grin (Ms. D. does love the democratic process). After a burst of static hissed itself out of the mic, Paige coughed, smoothed a hank of hair out of her eyes, and leaned forward.

"What do you know about the rumored sale of Everett Field?"

Uh, this *so* had nothing to do with Smart Water.

Onstage, Logan's smile faltered momentarily. I may have been the only one to notice. He tapped at his mic and was rewarded with a screech of feedback, causing Shelby to actually turn around and face forward for more than three seconds at a time.

Logan leaned into his microphone, which, tellingly, had finally decided to behave. There was nary a pop or crackle to be heard.

"I can answer that," he said, blasting everyone within a fifteen-row radius with the full effect of his electric-blue irises. He should patent those, peddle their genetic coding for a profit, no joke.

"Keep in mind that everything is still being

negotiated," Logan began smoothly, sounding like someone who ought to be toting a leather brief-case and doing said negotiations himself. I almost swooned, he was being so mature and leadery. "But the school board has been approached with an offer for the land."

"We can't sell that land! It's . . . *historic*!" Paige sput-tered, looking outraged. Paige is about five feet tall and twig-skinny, so outrage looked slightly absurd on her. But her flashing eyes conveyed her emotions loud and clear.

At that moment, I thought that Paige was maybe being disloyal. Little did I know that I was about to fol-low her lead.

"True," Logan said, folding his arms in front of him, "but the money would go toward funding a new arts program, which would attract more stu-dents from out of district. And more attention from college ranking systems. So the sale could be a good thing."

"The money could come from somewhere else," Paige pointed out, obviously not willing to concede all that easily.

Logan shrugged. Lord, even his shrugging was sexy. Boy's got some shoulders on him, what can I say?

"It could, I suppose. But the truth is, as important as Everett Field is to us as a student body" — and here he took a moment to flash some dimpley goodness my way in a subtle gesture meant only for the two of us — "this is really a decision for the school board, not the student council."

And there it was again. The reason we were going to just roll over and let Everett Field — and Edwina St. Claire, my writing fantasies, and my romantic memories with Logan — be bulldozed away to make room for a *gas station*, of all things.

I glanced up at the stage. Logan's expression had turned contemplative. It made me thoughtful myself.

"It's not like there's no precedent for student council getting involved in school board matters."

Wait. Did *I* say that?

No. Nu-uh. Surely not. I did not just contradict my boyfriend in the middle of his student council debate. I especially didn't *stand up* to do so. And how in the holy heck did I then find myself clutching the portable mic — *thank you, Ms. Donatello* — white-knuckling my way into an extremely awkward exchange with a bemused-looking Logan?

"You don't think we'd benefit from a new arts program?" he asked, the slight hitch in his voice giving him away. He wasn't pleased with this turn of events.

"Of course we would," I agreed quickly. "I'm just saying, we could probably find that money some other way."

"It's not that simple," Logan said, starting to look a little peevish. "It's not that easy to scrape together money like that."

"I mean, I know we don't really know exactly how much money's involved here," I said — how was I even still speaking? What alien force had kidnapped my body? But yeah, I still had the floor, literally and figuratively. "But —"

And looking back, this was *it*. 2:48 P.M. The moment that I totally sold my boyfriend down the river. Whoever this alien was that had body-snatched me, he/she/it was totally looking to throw down —

"*We could try*, right? If it were something that you believed in?"

Utter silence. No one could believe the words that had just come out of my mouth. Not even me. Heresy, treason, evil on par with full-fat ice cream.

But I wasn't. Even. Done. Yet.

"Right?"

Right.

☆ ☆ ☆ ☆ ☆

It's 6:48 P.M., four hours after the debate debacle, which, although kind of fun to say out loud, was excruciating on a level previously unknown to me in my entire two-year history as Logan's girlfriend.

I'm not sure what to do with myself. Dad's working late and Mom is at a spin class. I'm not thrilled about having the house to myself in these desperate times. I actually almost went with Mom to the gym, which just goes to show you how frantic I'm feeling for some distraction, but at the last second I came to my senses. I mean – the *gym*. And here I was looking to try to feel better.

I think my senses may have steered me wrong, though, because ever since Mom left, all I've been able to do is to sit in my bedroom, curled up on the overstuffed window seat, staring blankly outside like some kind of electroshock therapy patient.

Would it really have been so difficult just to stick to the rehearsed questions? Themed proms, fortified water products . . . they were no-brainers. That was to say, they would have required no brains. They would have required less brainpower than it took for me to completely toss reason and loyalty out the window.

My cell phone rings. John Mayer. It's Logan.

"Hey," I say.

"Erin."

"That's me."

No reply. Okay, this is not a time for jokey teasing. I get that.

"You're annoyed." Apparently this *is* a time for stating the obvious.

Logan inhales sharply. "You could say that." He pauses. "Maybe I'm more confused. Erin, were you *trying* to make me look bad up there?"

"No! Of course not!" I wave my hands frantically, then realize he can't see them over the phone. "Look, I didn't mean to go off script like that. You know I'm not a go-off-script kind of girl."

"I do know. Well, I thought I knew."

"I guess Everett Field is just a touchy subject for me."

It is. I think back to all of the sunny Sunday afternoons I've spent there. Yeah, the place has sentimental value. But it's not just sentiment, it's *history*. Doesn't the school board see that? Doesn't Logan?

Doesn't my boyfriend understand me?

I think back to when he squeezed my hand the other day, sitting beside me on the park bench. What happened to that Logan? Prince Charming Logan? Where did he go?

"They're building a gas station, Erin, not a nuclear power plant." Is he whining? Is that a whine I hear? "It means more revenue for the town."

"Isn't there anywhere else for Caswell to build a gross gas station?" I demand.

Why do I care so much about this?

"The school needs the money!" Logan sounds exasperated. My gut reaction is to remind him that there are other ways to raise the money, but I swallow, hard.

This is supposed to be my grovel-fest.

I decide to let it go. I tell myself it's only for now.

"I was wrong," I say.

Shocked silence.

"Yeah?" He's holding out.

I sigh. I slip back into the role that fits me like a glove. "I made it sound like I wasn't supporting your platform or your point of view. I was way off. You know that's not the way it is."

"O-okay." He waits for more.

I throw dignity to the winds. "You know I'm completely your number one fan," I tell him. "I'm the First Girlfriend!"

"You are." He says this like he's maybe reconsidering my eligibility for the position. He's going to reopen the girlfriend polls or something.

53

"Listen, you still killed at the debate. There are plenty of kids who totally agree with your point of view. If anything, I came off looking totally possessed."

He laughs, and suddenly I'm not sure that I want him to. He's running unopposed, after all. It's possible he's overreacting. "Fair enough. You did look kind of nuts."

"Don't worry, Logan. There's no way that I damaged your campaign. You've got the popular vote totally, completely, and one hundred percent wrapped up."

This seems to placate him. He sighs with resignation.

"I hope so."

It's not exactly "I love you," but I'll take it, for now.

Today I acted out of character. After two years of unwavering Logan fandom, two years of listening brightly (no pun intended) while he practiced his campaign speeches, two years of posters, slogans, and celebratory Twizzlers, I finally stuck my foot in my mouth.

As Caleb Bright's daughter, I know from putting your best foot forward (as opposed to, for example, down one's own throat). Sure, sometimes I wish I could be a little bit more rebellious, but punky hair dye, visible piercings in places other than earlobes, and conspicuous tattoos are not for the daughter of the mayor. My hair is long and ironed. My fingernails are neat and filed. My trouser-legged jeans are actually professionally pressed. I am straight. And narrow. And I always know exactly what a situation calls for.

Until today.

See, the thing is, as much as questioning Logan — *challenging* Logan — seemed like completely un-Erin behavior, maybe the real issue is what exactly "Erin behavior" truly is.

Acting out of character today meant admitting that sometimes I don't enjoy feeling buttoned-up. When I'm stretched out with a magazine in Everett Field, I ditch the trouser jeans for stretchy velour track pants. The headband comes off, the hair fans out, and I wiggle my bare toes in a thick blanket of grass. Speaking out on behalf of Everett Field was me admitting that the place is special to me, important. Admitting that being at Everett Field puts me in touch with other sides of myself. Sides that I keep hidden, not just from my friends but from myself.

Maybe today, I wasn't so much acting out of character as I was finally *getting in touch with* my character, for one of the first times in my life.

Maybe.

Am I sorry for upsetting the debate? For upsetting Logan? Of course. But that doesn't mean I'm sorry for caring about the field. It takes *strength* of character to be able to be both, I think.

Comments (1)

By the_book: Wowza — who know you had it in ya, Brightgirl? Well said.

A2Z: seriously? *what* r u going on about these days? do u need to borrow those crystal earrings my mom got me from Belize that are all supposed to balance your internal energy? i know we said they were hokey, but who knows? it really, really sounds like your internal energy could use some balancing.

Sigh. Zoë clearly has no patience for my spontane-ous leave of sanity. But this By_the_book person seems kind of into the emerging, unbalanced Erin.

If only I knew who he or she was . . .

☆ Chapter Five

Crisp air tickles skin.
Rays of sunshine warm the bones.
No gas station here.

Okay, no.

I close my notebook with resignation and re-cap my pen. What can I say? There's a reason I'm a blogger and not so much a poet.

Now that my morning writing session is kaput, I whip out my knockoff Prada wraparound sunglasses and slide them on. I wasn't joking about the sunshine. My bones, they are warm.

And the air is crisp and sweet, like early fall, just before the weather turns and we all have to start bundling into extra layers. The trees that surround Everett Field blaze autumnal, leaves lapping at the sky in a fiery-hued tapestry.

They really want to put a gas station *here*? It's insane.

I just can't let it happen.

☆ ☆ ☆ ☆ ☆

"We need to talk."

Those four words are always portentous, but I hardly expect to be hearing them from my girlfriends instead of a boyfriend. Still, yup — here's Shelby, bearing down on me, and Zoë scowling. Something is amiss in the halls of Plainsboro High. Something to do with me.

"Yes?" I say lightly. I push aside the English lit essay I've been reviewing during my study period.

Shelby and Zoë have tracked me down in the least likely of places, aka the library. It seems like I spent a tad too much time on nonrequired writing last night to give my actual homework the polish it needed. Unacceptable. If sagging grades don't give me away, the purplish shadows underlining my eyes will.

Très chic.

"What is up with you and Logan?" Shelby asks, worry flashing in her eyes. She settles into a seat across from me at my table and dumps her extremely adorable fringed hobo bag down at her side.

60

"Seriously." Zoë settles in next to Shelby.

Unlike Z, Shelby seems to have asked an actual question, so I cap my turquoise Pilot ultra-fine-point pen and turn my attention to her.

"We're fine." I frown. "Okay, maybe not one hundred and thirty percent fine, but, you know, we're okay." Pause. "We talked."

I fiddle with the pen cap, twist it back and forth, realize what I'm doing, and drop the pen back onto the tabletop.

"I apologized last night for throwing the debate off track. He gets it. I mean, I don't think he's going to be planning me a surprise serenade anytime soon, but, you know, it's cool." I think. I *hope*.

"*Really,*" Zoë says. Again, it's not quite a question, so I glance over at her and shrug.

"Erin," Shelby levels with me, "he saw the blog."

"The blog?"

What does she mean, he saw it? It's not, like, a big secret or anything. I mean, it's online. So he saw it. So what?

She nods grimly. "He's not happy."

Zoë shakes her head like she can't believe me. Maybe she really can't.

"There was nothing wrong with that post," I say, feeling defensive. My chest is hot and I'm sure my

61

cheeks are pink. "I apologized to Logan. I was just sort of explaining where I was coming from."

Why is this whole thing getting so blown out of proportion?

"But then you had to go and get all weird about the field, how being in the park is, like, the essence of your character," Zoë says. Now she's scowling again. For a pretty girl, she sure can work a scowl. Yeesh.

The back of my throat goes dry and prickly. "That wasn't weird, Z," I say slowly, "that was honest."

I swear, I didn't think my post was any kind of big exposé. The only people who even read my blog are Shelby, Zoë, Logan, sometimes Theo and Paige, and maybe a handful of kids from student council and stuff. I don't post anything up there that I wouldn't say to their faces. In fact, I think I kind of was, basically, posting to their faces. In the hopes that they would maybe read it and see where I was coming from.

Those hopes were in vain, obviously.

"It was nice of you to apologize," Shelby says finally, pursing her orange-tinted, glossy lips together. She's the only redhead I know who can pull off tangerine lip tint. "But I don't think Logan saw the post that way. I think he felt kind of betrayed by you waxing all nostalgic about Everett Field — especially since you got all up in his face about it during the debate."

My stomach hitches like a stalled motor engine. "How do you know any of this? Did you talk to Logan?" There's no way that she talked to Logan. That would just be weird. And a little bit backstabby.

She shakes her head no, digs a bottle of Diet Coke out of her bag, twists the cap off, sips. "Tripp told me."

Great, one more person involved in this drama. I should be grateful for the heads-up, I guess. "I'll find him. I'll talk to him." Soon, I hope. This mini-crisis is starting to take on a life of its own.

The bell rings. Geometry. I can't make sense of anything in my life right now; how in the heck am I going to handle proofs, theorems, and intersecting lines?

Intersecting — that's the problem. Logan and I are totally not intersecting. We are parallel planes. Extending in opposite directions. This is no good.

"I'll talk to him," I repeat. "Later."

For now, I'm late to class.

☆ ☆ ☆ ☆ ☆

Math's never been my best subject, so factoring Logan stress into the equation pretty much means that trigonometry class is lost on me. I spend forty-three minutes doodling my initials into my notebook. By the time

63

class ends, I've got at least twenty-seven versions of my signature down cold. I'm thrilled, relieved, and a little bit sweaty when it's finally over.

The good news about fourth period is that it's when Logan's and my schedules coincide such that we flit past each other on our way toward our respective English electives (me: The Modern Memoir; him: Contemporary American Heroes). We're two literary ships passing in a crowded hallway.

Maybe it's *too* crowded. I think I can make out the sleeve of his favorite suede jacket but . . . or, no, that might be the tip of a brown curl . . .

Yeah, okay, it's him.

I wave, but he doesn't see me. He has his head down like he's concentrating very intently on counting the scratched linoleum floor tiles.

"Logan!" Now that I can see the full explosion of his rumpled brown curls I quicken my pace, tilt my head, and grin at him hopefully. "Hey."

He stops short in front of me, looking one part surprised, two parts irritated. I realize suddenly that it wasn't so much as he'd been intently staring at the floor as that he'd been intently *not* staring at me. His not-gaze speaks volumes. Shelby was right. For that matter, so was Zoë, though she was a little bit meaner about it.

"Haven't seen you today," I say, aiming for "breezy" but face-planting somewhere closer to "painfully obvious and awkward." I am suddenly aware that I am standing a hair too close to him given that we're clearly not on smooch-tastic terms.

Finally, he looks directly at me. Ouch. I sort of wish he hadn't. Evidently the power of those radiant eyes can be harnessed for evil as well as for good.

"Yeah." He clears his throat and, I swear, it sounds louder than a garbage disposal. "Well. I, uh, haven't really wanted to see you."

Double, extra, venti-ouch, with a shot of *oooh* thrown in for good measure. My ego needs an Ace bandage.

"If you're upset about the blog —" I start, as though I haven't just had a full blow-by-blow briefing of the situation with my two best friends.

"You know what?" he says, cutting me off, dropping his eyes to some point on the horizon far over my shoulder and out of my sightline. "Don't. Not now."

"Okay," I say, faltering. "But —"

"*Erin.*" Now he puts his hand on my forearm, very *I'm serious.* As opposed to, say, *I'm totally over this dumbness,* so at least that's a slight silver lining.

Right?

"Just don't."

My silver lining goes all cloudy and black.

And then he's gone, down the hall, walking away.

It doesn't even matter whether he's looking at the floor tiles again; by now, I can't see his face anymore, anyway.

☆ ☆ ☆ ☆ ☆

I need a plan, stat. Thankfully, I'm pretty good at plans. Chalk it up to all those years hanging around campaign headquarters while everyone was being all high-stress and strategic.

I'm especially lucky today because I have a free period for my last class. Normally this means I can cut out early and go home, but today I'm a flurry of candles, blankets, and yummy finger foods like crackers, fruit, cheese, and chocolate. I'm like a gourmand Tasmanian devil.

I intercept Logan right in front of his locker. He's calmed down since our last encounter. I guess the last bell of the day will do that to a guy.

"Hey," he says, giving me a sheepish one-armed hug. "Sorry about before."

"No, I am," I say, shaking my head. "Of course you were annoyed." Hearing him say "I'm sorry" reawakens the Mexican jumping beans in my stomach again; this time they're leaping, turning cartwheels in my throat. I just want things to be right between us.

"Well, I'm over it," he assures me.

"Good." I link my arm through his. "I have a surprise for you."

His eyes widen. "I like surprises."

All at once, it feels like we're us again, Erin and Logan, happy and perfect and cute and in love. I can breathe.

"I know you do."

☆ ☆ ☆ ☆ ☆

It doesn't take a whole lot of persuading to get Logan blindfolded and into the shotgun seat of my car (see previous note re: surprises, and his relative appreciation for). I drive into town and do a few laps down Main Street just to throw him off track, then double back to school, where I pull around to the back parking lot and kill the engine.

"Come on." I take Logan's hand and wander forward. I don't know why I'm feeling so tentative; I'm not the one who doesn't know where we're going.

"Smells like parking lot," Logan observes. He

wiggles his nose. It's pretty cute, so I plant a light kiss on the tip of it.

"You're not wrong."

We stop, Logan stumbling slightly. I stand on tip-toes and unknot his blindfold with a flourish.

"Ta-da!" I do another of my signature jazz hands for the sake of presentation.

Logan steps back and blinks, taking in the scene.

We're at Everett Field, of course. What better way to make amends than to reclaim the controversial territory for our own again?

I've laid out a bedsheet to serve as a picnic blanket (it's an old Strawberry Shortcake number from when I was, like, eight, which is slightly embarrassing but also probably won't be missed by Mom), and on top of that there's a stuffed-to-the-brim basket of munchies. I've also plunked down some scented candles, which are not lit yet (safety first!).

All in all, it's a darn romantic scene.

I turn to Logan expectantly. It's all I can do not to leap into his arms. Obviously he's going to completely melt from the schmoopy loviness of it all.

You can imagine, then, my shock to see the corners of his mouth stretch tight and his eyes glint with frustration. He looks dubious.

No, he looks *furious*.

Logan glances at me. You know that expression "if looks could kill"? Well, um, yeah.

"Is this a joke, Erin?" he asks.

Is he kidding? A romantic picnic in Everett Field? A joke? Of course it's not a joke. I stare at him, startled.

He's not kidding.

"I thought..." I trail off. I don't even know what I thought. Maybe I thought that he was my boyfriend before he was "Logan Tanner: PHS President." But clearly I thought wrong.

"The field is sort of a sore topic, babe," he says.

He shakes his head, and I don't know if it's my frustration at having every single gesture of mine completely and totally misinterpreted over the last few days, but something in me sort of snaps. Like I can hear it, a little cracking sound coming from somewhere deep behind my solar plexus.

"Well, maybe it wouldn't be such a sore topic if you would just *chill out* for a minute," I say. Then I step back, surprised by my own anger.

Logan is pretty taken aback, too. "Nice, Erin," he says, his annoyance clearly growing. "Maybe you should try putting yourself in someone else's shoes for a little while. Do you have any idea of the pressure involved in being student council president?"

69

I laugh. I don't mean to, this is so absolutely the wrong time for laughter, but, I mean — is he out of his ever-loving *mind*? "No," I say, deadpan. "No idea."

"Right." He rolls his eyes. "Because of your father. News flash, Erin: You're not your father. You're just an accessory to his campaign."

Tell me he didn't just say that out loud.

Even Logan looks like maybe he thinks he just crossed a line, but his anger has gotten rolling now, feeding on itself. "You have no idea what the *actual* spotlight is like. You couldn't handle it."

I snort. "Logan, all I *do* is handle it." Now I'm good and riled up, too. How dare he? Like he's had to ever spend even one second under public scrutiny the way my mother and I do? Like he's ever experienced any real, honest, grown-up pressure with actual stakes involved? Like he's ever tiptoed around, trying to be perfect, hoping that nothing you do gets you or your family in trouble?

"If you think I'm just an accessory," I say, "*you* can find yourself a new one."

Logan's mouth drops open. Now, for the first time, he looks uncertain. "Oh, come on, Er," he says, back-tracking slightly. "Maybe you're overreacting."

"Am I?" I sweep my eyes across the tableau I've laid

out: the candles, the food, the dancing Strawberry Shortcakes. What was the point?

Logan may be smart, funny, popular, and cute, but right now he is also proving himself to be kind of a jerk.

"Go for it," I tell him, the blood pounding in my ears. "Replace me. Or, try to. Because I'm done here."

So I walk away.

☆ ☆ ☆ ☆ ☆

"What do you think of this?"

Mom holds a dress up for my inspection. It's a pale, dusty rose satin, ruched down the front, with a slightly A-line skirt. It's . . . gorgeous, actually.

"I like." I give her a thumbs-up from where I'm stretched out on my bed.

I've been curled up in here, laptop propped open next to me, notebook strewn at my feet, trying to make sense of my thoughts ever since that ick-tastic fight with Logan. It's not working. There's no sense to be made. The dress is a nice distraction. Even though —

"What's it for?" I ask. I think for a moment, biting at my lower lip. Have I forgotten about some First

71

Daughter public appearance? That would be so unlike me.

Mom smiles, her eyes crinkling in that graceful way that she has. "I saw it today, while I was out at lunch, and it looked like it would suit you. So I grabbed it. Just in case." She crosses her slender fingers with the hand that's not holding the dress.

"In case they suddenly decide to hold the prom over winter break?" I'm still puzzled.

She shakes her head at me. "In case your dad wins." She winks. "*In case.*" Her fingers are still crossed.

"Ah, we're planning ahead." I nod. We do that sometimes.

"Yes. And I was thinking that I could probably swing by Bloomingdale's, see if they have a tie in a similar shade. Something Logan could wear that would pick up the shadows in the dress's silhouette . . ." She trails off when she notices my dark expression.

"I wouldn't count on Logan playing dress-up for us," I warn her. "Things are . . . weird. We had a thing. A fight thing." There. It's out. Admitting it is the first step, right?

"What about?" She hooks the dress hanger over my door and quickly crosses the room, settling next to me on the bed with a worried look.

I shrug. "We don't see eye to eye on some stuff. His platform."

Now her eyebrows shoot up. "His platform?" she asks, like I've just told her that Logan and I don't see eye to eye on not lying facedown in a pile of wet sand for prolonged periods of time. Then the corners of her mouth prick up like she's trying not to laugh. "What, does he want to hire a dj for the winter semiformal out of the student council budget?"

"I guess it's complicated," I say, unsure. I'm frustrated that I can't help her see things my way. I'm frustrated by how badly I want to.

She pats me on the shoulder, the flat of her palm warm but strong. "It's not, Erin," she says. "Not unless you make it that way."

☆ ☆ ☆ ☆ ☆

"*What* is the drama?" Zoë sniffs at me across our table at the diner like she's smelling something foul. She swipes a fry off of my plate. "And why didn't you get your usual?" She means because I decided to forgo the American cheese on my french fries.

"I'm not feeling like my usual self," I understate.

"Obviously." She sniffs, then stares down at her cell phone and starts punching keys.

Since my fight with Logan, I have been unsuccessful in my quest to get *anyone* to see things my way. My mom was a washout, and also completely MIA after our little non-heart-to-heart. I blame the gym. Or maybe she even went out shopping for Logan. Who knows? Hope springs eternal.

I recruited Shelby and Zoë into a late-night diner session, but it hasn't exactly been like old times. Though maybe that's my fault for not getting the cheese fries.

"Obvs you're all bunched up about the field, Er," Shelby says, daintily spreading jelly on the stump of her decapitated corn muffin. "But I don't see why you have to sacrifice your relationship over the whole deal."

I take a swig of Diet Coke before answering. It doesn't calm me. "He called me an *accessory*," I growl, feeling dangerously close to crying.

"Okay," Z offers, "but was he, like, calling you a diamond tennis bracelet? Or CZ studs? 'Cause there's a difference."

If my eyes were opened any wider, I think they'd swallow the booth up whole.

Z laughs. "Gawd, Erin, if you're going to be so freaked about this whole thing, you should just save the field on your own. You know . . . run against Logan." She does her best impression of an Uncle Sam poster.

Hold on.

She might be on to something.

The truth is, the main reason that Logan's been student council president for the past two years is because he's never once been up against a viable candidate.

And suddenly, I realize something: All that's about to change. Hell hath no fury like an accessory scorned.

I am a viable candidate. In every way. *I'm* going to go up against Logan. My *ex*-boyfriend, Logan.

And I'm going to kick his butt.

http://firstgirlbright.blogorama.com

September 22, 11:55 pm

You can call me Madam President. President Bright.

Ms. President Erin to you.

Comments (1)

By_the_book: Best news I've heard all day. Let the games begin, Prez-ette!

☆ Chapter Six

By the time I get in bed that night, my plan of world domination (well, PHS domination, but it's sort of the same thing, in this situation) is starting to seem like maybe not the smartest plan I've ever had. Lying in bed, staring up at the ceiling, I can't help but replay the Erin and Logan greatest hits reel through my mind: our first picnic at Everett Field, i.e., the one that actually went well; the first time he ever gave me a Valentine's Day card ("Every day, I love you . . . a little mower," with a picture of a lawn mower on the front — how cute!); our first tooth-clanking, nose-bumping, toe-curling, awkward/amazing/electric first kiss . . .

What can I say? I love Logan. Being furious with him hasn't changed that.

I'm tempted to call him, to tell him that I'm sorry and I've made a huge mistake.

(Well, two huge mistakes, technically, between

breaking up with him and announcing my plan to run for student council president. Or maybe even four huge mistakes, if you include the debate and the blog post. But really, who's counting?)

I sit up in bed, pushing down my Nick & Nora cotton sleep-shirt where it's all bunched up at my hips. I'm sweaty and not at all tired.

I flip the switch on my bedside lamp. It casts a glow over my nightstand that feels otherworldly and ethereal. Or maybe that's just the exhaustion talking.

My cell phone sits atop my nightstand. Its purple glitter cover twinkles at me invitingly.

Call Logan . . . Call Logan . . . Call Logan . . .

Instead, I remind myself I've already posted on my blog about running for president, which Logan has definitely seen, and which I definitely can't take back.

I remind myself, too, that there's nothing respectable about letting your boyfriend walk all over you. And then the urge to call him — or gorge on peanut butter Hershey's Kisses while listening to female folk-singers — passes. Chocolate does terrible things to my skin, so that's an added plus of my newfound willpower.

☆ ☆ ☆ ☆ ☆

Ten minutes later, my willpower crumbles. I'm hunched over the kitchen counter, excavating huge chunks of cookie dough from some low-fat frozen yogurt, when the overhead light clicks on harshly, making me blink.

"Erin?" Mom blinks, too. Her face is ghostly pale, free of makeup and slick with expensive night cream. Her eyes dart toward the yogurt.

Midnight snacks = not cool.

"I couldn't sleep," I say by way of apology, putting the lid back on the yogurt and replacing it in the freezer.

"It's late," she says.

I'm about to burst out with it — running for student council president, going up against Logan via my blog — when she jerks her head in the direction of the counter.

"Rinse your spoon and put it in the dishwasher before you get back in bed," she tells me, then pads off to her own bedroom.

☆ ☆ ☆ ☆ ☆

When I wake in the morning, I realize I'm going to need a double dose of my Clinique concealer. But I realize something else, too: I *totally* want to run against

Logan for PHS student council president. I absolutely and completely do want to trounce him. And I believe that I can.

Unfortunately for me, first I have to deal with the small matter of getting my name on the ballot.

Which is easier said than done.

☆ ☆ ☆ ☆ ☆

"It's allowed," I tell Ms. Donatello fervently. "I mean, I'm sure of it." Ninety-nine percent sure, anyway. Or at least ninety-six.

Ms. Donatello may be cool, but she's still a teacher. Which means she's a stickler for rules.

"You want to . . . run? For president?" she asks me, looking incredibly confused.

As student council advisor, Ms. D. oversees the election. So I make it my business to hunt her down first thing Thursday morning.

It's clear to me that her disbelief works on two levels: first, that I want to run, despite the fact that the window for announcing candidacy closed a good two weeks ago.

There's also the fact that up until yesterday afternoon, I was PHS's most staunchly pro-Logan advocate.

"Yup," I say. I compose myself in what I hope is a very presidential posture: shoulders back, stomach in, strong eye contact. I know all about the power of appearances (the plus side to having been groomed as an . . . *accessory*, I guess). I'm wearing my favorite heather-gray plaid A-line skirt with a raspberry-colored cable-knit sweater, dark gray tights, tall boots, and a wide headband. Plus my glasses. It's all very preppy and screams "Madam President!"

"Did something happen between you and Logan?"

"Yup." I look away but don't offer any more.

She seems to get it, sighing and running her fingers through her bangs. I notice that her fingernails are painted a deep indigo. They reflect the dull fluorescent lighting of the history classroom. She really does rock.

"The problem, Erin, is that candidates were supposed to announce their intention to run two weeks ago."

"I know that," I tell her. As if that's really the only thing going on here that's problematic. "Normally I wouldn't ask for favors, but . . ."

But I'm going to ask for a favor.

She folds her arms over her chest. "It's not even a question of whether or not you can ask. I don't think it's possible. I don't think it's *legal*."

I raise an eyebrow at her. I think we both know that no one's going to be making any kind of citizen's arrest if she bends the rules for me. That would be extreme.

"I don't think it's kosher," she amends.

"There are . . . extenuating circumstances," I say, a little bit desperate.

"Such as . . ." She's excited about a race that actually exploits the democratic process. She likes that. She wants someone to run against Logan, for a change. She's really not buying this — but she wants to. I can tell. She likes *me*. I'm likable. That's why I'm going to be able to do this — all of this.

"The situation with the school board and Everett Field," I say, in a burst of inspiration. "That's new."

"That also doesn't fall under the purview of the student council," Ms. D. reminds me wryly.

"But it *should*," I insist. "And that's going to be my platform. I'm going to protest the sale of Everett Field. I'm going to raise the money for the arts program in some other way."

She bites her lower lip thoughtfully. "There's a thing . . ."

"A thing would be great!" I seize on this elusive "thing" of which she speaks. *Love* "things."

"*If* extenuating circumstances arise —"

82

"Everett Field —" I singsong softly, looking at Ms. D. meaningfully.

"Yes, that would count," she admits. "If extenuating circumstances arise, a candidate can lobby to enter the race if he or she can gather signatures from twenty-five percent of the acting student council body."

Twenty-five percent? That's, like, six people. I can do twenty-five percent. I can do twenty-five percent in my sleep. I can especially do it in my lucky raspberry sweater.

"Done," I say decisively, holding out my hand for Ms. Donatello to shake. I'm hoping some of her nail polish grunge-glamour will rub off on me (metaphorically, that is. Indigo nails would really not go with this outfit).

"You've got twenty-four hours," she tells me. "And I have to warn you —"

"It may be harder than you think," I fill in, then smile at her. What was it I was saying before about an accessory scorned?

☆ ☆ ☆ ☆ ☆

The smell of wet flour and soggy newspaper tells me I've found Missy Jackson.

Honestly, I don't know why everyone's so bent out

of shape about a new arts program. Missy is a crafts *fiend*, and often spends her lunch period in the art room working on something crazy and out there. Like today, for instance, I track her down as she applies long strips of pasty paper to the front side of an oblong balloon.

"Papier mâché?" I pull a plastic chair on over to where she's working, wincing as its aluminum legs scrape against the floor.

"Yup." She grins proudly. "Masks. For the winter semiformal decorations."

The winter semiformal is, like, three months away. But, okay.

"Cool," I say, scooting my chair in closer. I lower my voice conspiratorially. "So, Missy," I begin, ever so casual, "have you ever had a look at my blog . . . ?"

☆ ☆ ☆ ☆ ☆

"You. Are out of your mind."

My locker door clangs shut with a metallic clanking sound, and for a second Shelby almost looks like she feels bad for sneaking up on me.

Almost.

"Hey, Shelby. Love your jeans — are they new?" I decide to ignore her comment and go straight for the girl talk. I think the jeans are Miss Sixty. They're really cute, with whiskered thighs and full, wide legs.

She leans against my locker and shakes her head at me, her lips pursed tightly. "Flattery will get you nowhere. Don't try to change the subject, girlfriend."

"*Ex*-girlfriend," I correct her, holding one finger up in a schoolmarmish pose.

She frowns. If she presses her lips together any more forcefully, they'll disappear right up into her face. "Right."

"Are you having PMS?" Zoë chimes in, clearly irritated by the unseemliness of this all. She peeks her head just over Shelby's shoulder. They're like the angel and the devil sitting on my shoulders, whispering in my ears. Except I'm not sure which is which, and honestly — whispering would be a welcome shift in behavior. They seem to be ganging up on me. This is headed nowhere good, and fast.

"Well — no," I stammer. "But I hate it when people blame problems on *that*."

"So this is a new-wave feminist thing you've got going," Z says, puckering her mouth up at the taste of the word *feminist*. This from a girl who thinks feminism is getting your hair cut above your shoulders.

I roll my eyes. "Right. Girls aren't supposed to be

85

student council presidents." I wave a sheet of paper in their direction. "But I've got six signatures here that say otherwise." In addition to five committee members who, it turns out, are almost as dedicated to Everett Field as I am, Missy Jackson, bless her, came through in a pinch.

"So you're really going through with this?" Zoë asks, looking increasingly grossed out.

I nod. Her reaction is only fueling my fire. "Absolutely. I think it would be nuts for us not to at least *try* to lobby to keep the field around, *and* in the school's possession. But also? Logan's gotten cocky. He needs to know that he's not the only one who can lead the PHS student body."

I mean it, I realize, and as I'm speaking, my voice takes on the clear, confident intonation of sincerity. I've heard the same thing happen to my father at countless debates. It's a good sign, the intonation; it means you're being persuasive.

And it usually means you're going to win.

Unfortunately, I can tell that I'm doing nothing to bring Zoë and Shelby around to my way of thinking. My persuasion has limited reach right now.

"It's social suicide," Zoë says, cracking down hard on a piece of gum, like if she gnaws away with enough intensity, she'll convince me to change my mind. I'm just worried that her jaws are going to literally unhinge.

I glance at Shelby. So far, she seems like the one more likely to be sympathetic. But the look in her eyes says that she's riding the same train as Zoë, and that both of them are seriously convinced I'm headed for self-destructionville.

For the second time in as many days, I falter. Ugh. "You'll . . . vote for me, won't you?"

The back of my throat feels scratchy and hot. It's not possible that my girls would just abandon me right now, is it? I mean, I'm going through a breakup. I need them now more than ever.

And besides — what about all we've been through together? Like when my first dog, Marshmallow, ran away, and we put up a zillion posters in the neighborhood, until some weird kid from one town over returned her and we decided to get her microchipped? Or when Shelby's parents got divorced and we had sleepover parties every weekend and watched episodes of *Lizzie McGuire* and tried on all of my mother's old lipsticks? Or that time Zoë got that botched eyebrow wax and we banded together to pencil her in some new ones so she could go on her big date with Chuck Preston? We gave her *eyebrows.*

"We already told Logan that we were voting for him," Zoë says, smashing my heart into smithereens. "We *promised*."

I glare at her, her perfectly arched, professionally tweezed, pristine eyebrows and all. I wish I had an eyebrow pencil that I could use to scribble an evil villain moustache on her face. Not that it would do much good.

I put my hands on my hips and look at Shelby, challenging her. She flinches, but she holds my gaze.

"He's counting on us," she says. Like Logan would even know if they switched their votes. Please. The ballots are anonymous. "Allie Soren's working on his campaign," she adds as an afterthought, knowing as she says it that it's like another knife to my chest.

"*I* was counting on you," I say. I shut my locker door with a clang and spin on my heels, all the better to flounce off indignantly.

I *was* counting on them. Really, extra, super counting on them. That was my fifth official huge mistake.

Yes, you got me — I was still counting. And I had a feeling things weren't going to get much better anytime soon.

Later, I check my blog again.

http://firstgirlbright.blogorama.com
September 23, 4:55 pm

You can call me Madam President. President
Bright.

Ms. President Erin to you.

<u>Comments (17)</u>
Sby16: really not sure about this 1. Don't shoot the
messenger.

TeddyB: Winds of change! *Quel scandal!*

Miss_Mindy: Could be time for some fresh blood
on the PHS council. Bsides, I heart Everett Field.

Asoren: Gawd, are you all *socialists* or something?
Sell the freaking field and let's all move on.

DeathbyCommittee: Has Prince Logan weighed in on any of this yet?

Asoren: Not a word. Shocking. Guess that relationship's done. Good news for all of you First Chica wannabes!

By_the_book: Best news I've heard all day. Let the games begin, Prez-ette!

I shut the computer before I can see any more of the comments. I guess I never realized how many people read my blog. Some are obvious, of course. TeddyB is Theo; Miss_Mindy is Mindy Jackson. Asoren is Allie Soren, and I'm not sure, but I'm guessing that DeathbyCommittee is her little sidekick troll, Diana Mark.

My stomach feels heavy, like I swallowed a bowling ball. There are some supporters of my decision, like the mysterious By_the_Book, and also a few students who are mostly intrigued by the gossip factor of the situation, but plenty of people have not-so-nice words for me. It doesn't go unnoticed that two of those plenty are my supposed BFFs.

"Dinner, Erin!" my mother calls to me from where I've been huddled on the couch in our family room, wrapped underneath a chenille throw blanket and crouched over my laptop. I'm not hungry in the least — and seriously doubt that any food will fit in around the aforementioned bowling ball — but family dinners are nonnegotiable. And I think some distraction might be nice.

I slide into my place at our kitchen table and help myself to some pesto-basil mashed potatoes from the local gourmet restaurant. (We often order in.) But I don't really want them and mostly just shove them back and forth on my plate with my fork.

"Something wrong, sweetie?" my mom asks, glancing at my restless fork syndrome. It isn't like me to totally disregard basic table manners.

"Uh." I'm not quite sure how to break it to the parents that I've suddenly gone all Ms. Politica, but they're going to find out sooner or later.

I decide the direct approach is the best tactic. I look up from my potatoes and try to smile. "I'm running for student council president."

"Erin!" My father grins so widely that I think his smile is going to fall right off his face and onto his plate. "That's so exciting!" He pats me on the shoulder heartily. I guess I never realized that he might be interested in having me follow in his footsteps. It's never really come up before.

My mother, on the other hand, looks very worried. Her cheeks are sucked in like she just tasted lemon, and her forehead has little crinkles just above the space between her eyebrows. "Isn't Logan running again this year?" she asks carefully.

I flush. "Yeah." I clear my throat. "Yes."

She raises her eyebrows now.

I cough. "Well, I told you. He and I just didn't see eye to eye on his platform," I say, reluctant to get into it again. The whole thing still feels totally surreal.

"Um, and we sort of argued about it. And things . . . deteriorated from there."

"So where do you two stand now?" she asks. Mom always liked Logan. She and Dad both did. What was there not to like? He is a parent's dream.

Also, she's been buying him clothes.

"I guess we're kind of . . . broken up."

"Oh, *Erin*," Mom says, actually placing her hand over her heart like she's a character in a soap opera.

This is so *not* what I need to hear. But what did I expect?

I don't know quite what I expected, but I can tell you for sure what I *didn't* expect: for my father to fully reach out across the table and envelop me in a crushing bear hug. "That's my girl," he says, sniffling slightly.

"Caleb — don't encourage her," my mom says. "They had a good thing. I'm not sure this is the best decision."

Neither am I, Mom. But it's too late to turn back now.

"Maggie, you're being unreasonable," my father protests. My stomach floods with relief, and for a moment, that bowling ball feels more like a beach ball. It's a slight improvement, but I will take it, for sure. "The girl is standing on principle. Sometimes that's what we need to do. It's a shame young people don't do that more often."

"Caleb —" She waves her butter knife at him, but he cuts her off.

"I'm sure this is all very exciting for Erin, but it's probably a little bit stressful, too. The last thing she needs is for us to give her grief."

I'll say.

He smiles at me again, his cheeks puffing up with pleasure and his chest puffing up with pride. He's very, very puffy all of a sudden. "I'm proud of you, Erin. I know you're going to run a stellar campaign."

"Thanks, Dad." I choke back the tiny sob that's working its way up my throat. The edges of my temples are brimming with the vibrations of his encouragement and my own doubt, and the combination is making me feel thick and dizzy.

I hope he's right that my campaign is going to rock. I really, truly hope that I'm going to be the next student council president of Plainsboro High. It's a big deal, you know.

And right this minute, I haven't got a whole lot else left.

☆ *Chapter Seven*

Monday afternoon is a student council informational meeting, where Ms. D. runs us through any upcoming events or announcements. Kind of a state of the union, if you will. This is the first one I am attending as a fellow candidate, rather than as Logan's number one groupie.

It's awkward.

I mean, some things are completely normal, like how this room still has that faint whiff of Carefree sugarless bubble gum to it from Ms. Espinoza's AP Spanish last period. That's something you can count on.

Not like ex-boyfriends.

Ex-boyfriends who are now casually sprawled out in a desk, khaki-clad legs splayed underneath, wearing casual-prep sneakers. Engaged in conversation with pinchy little Asoren.

The one good thing about being suddenly single and quasi-estranged from your friends, though, is that your weekends are really your own. So I'd had ample time to review my campaign strategy and also to emotionally prepare myself for this moment.

If only my emotions weren't suddenly so unreliable.

I blame Logan. It doesn't matter that I typed up an official-looking list of talking points on my computer, then spent an hour and thirty-three minutes memorizing them all. One look at Logan — who, in addition to wearing perfectly broken-in khakis, has also gotten a haircut over the weekend and looks extra adorable — and my carefully rehearsed points dissolve straight out of my skull. Looking at him sends my brain into overdrive; I can't decide if I want to kiss him or bang him over the head with my three-ring binder.

We are gathered in Ms. D.'s classroom. She's rearranged the desks into a big U shape, so that we can all see one another. Logan slumps back in his desk, ever casual, flanked on either side by Theo and Theo's friend Paige. And Allie Soren is close by, of course. I am perched opposite Logan, sitting stiffly in my seat and trying with all my might to project a confidence that, really, I'm not feeling at all.

I have no running mate. Again: awkward.

"So listen up, folks," Ms. Donatello begins, clapping her hands together purposefully as she settles herself Indian-style on top of her desk. "First off" — she waves an arm in my direction — "as some of you have already heard, we've got a new candidate joining the race. I think some of you may have petitioned to let her hop on. Good for you. So let's all welcome Erin."

Theo claps for me quietly and Paige nods toward me, but it's not exactly a ticker tape parade. Somewhere in the distance, I think I hear the chirping of crickets. I avoid meeting Logan's gaze.

"Tomorrow's our campaign fund-raising fair," she continues. "This is your opportunity to select a fund-raiser for your campaign. As the title of the fair would suggest." She smiles, poking a little bit of fun at herself. "Have you both given some thought to what your fund-raiser is going to be?"

Logan clears his throat and glances my way. "Car wash," he mumbles. I know that Logan could handle this campaign in his sleep, but it wouldn't necessarily kill him to look a touch more alive. I guess he really isn't too worried about the competition.

I wonder if I really think he should be.

"Great," Ms. Donatello says enthusiastically. She turns to me. "And our latecomer."

I blink, willing the salient bits of my talking points

97

back into my brain. Ah, yes — there they are! "A carnival," I say, mumbling slightly. I cough, clear my throat. "A carnival," I announce, more decisively this time. "And it won't be funds for my campaign or even for student council. I'm going to get it backed by local businesses, and I'm going to donate the money to the new arts program. That way, there's a chance that we'll be able to save Everett Field."

Ms. D. opens her mouth, then closes it again. Finally, she manages some actual words. "That's a pretty good idea," she admits, looking impressed and a little bit surprised. I decide to be flattered rather than to wonder why she's so shocked by my good-idea-having. "I think it's going to be a hit tomorrow with the rest of the students."

Tomorrow, we announce our fund-raisers in the hopes of encouraging the other students to help us plan and execute them. Normally I'm Logan's point person for all of his fund-raisy concerns. Normally. But there's nothing normal about this election.

I smile and shrug, consciously imitating Logan's cool, casual demeanor. I give a flip of my hair.

"I know," I say. "I'm counting on it."

☆ ☆ ☆ ☆ ☆

Whatever you might say about the student council presidential race, the fund-raising fair is one of those amazing things that tends to get you all warm and fuzzy and pro-school-spirit and stuff.

Yeah, I know I'm a huge nerd. I can't help it.

Last year, Logan organized a bake sale at our local community center. He was surrounded by little kids at all times. So cute.

Sigh.

This year, our tables are set on opposite sides of the auditorium. This year, we've each got our own sign-up sheet. This year, people can either choose to work with Logan or with me.

Part of me wishes that our tables were closer together, so I could see how many signatures he's gotten already. The other, more socially awkward part of me is relieved to have a little bit of breathing room.

The auditorium itself is warm and thick with humidity. Students wander back and forth, taking time to peruse our posters, ask questions, and swipe some chocolate (we're obviously not above low-level bribery).

A perky freshman that I recognize from homeroom stops in front of my table. "Hey." She smiles.

"Hi!" I slide a preprinted postcard across the table to her. "Are you interested in working on a carnival to raise money for our new arts program? If we can sell enough tickets, we might be able to convince the school board not to sell Everett Field." I tuck a strand of hair behind my ear and lean forward, pointing with a neatly polished index finger to some boldface print on the postcard.

She nods enthusiastically. "I am!" She has freckles on her cheeks that stretch outward when she smiles. "I'm so excited that we've got a female candidate running." Then she suddenly looks embarrassed. She's a freshman, of course she didn't realize. She hardly knows me, or Logan, for that matter. "I mean, Logan's great — or so everyone says —"

I save her. "Girl power!" I pump my fist at her.

"And the field . . ." She rolls her eyes. "A gas station? So crazy. It's a *historic site*!"

"I know," I reply. "Edwina St. Claire wrote —"

"*Restless Nature!*" she shrieks, cutting me off. She taps at her oversize denim tote bag. "I'm reading it right now."

"I'm always reading it. Well, rereading it," I admit.

"So, the fund-raisers are both next week?" she asks.

I nod.

"Great, count me in!" She signs her name with a flourish. This is the warmest anyone my age has been to me in days and I want to throw my arms around her. Luckily, I am able to hold myself back.

She caps her pen and waves good-bye. I allow myself a moment to sit back and feel pretty darn pleased with myself.

"Competition agrees with you. You look like you're having fun."

I nearly jump out of my seat. That's what I get for having a smug moment, I guess.

"Theo," I say, taking him in, "you scared me."

"Well, okay — you *looked* like you were having fun, until you looked like I had scared the bejeezus out of you." His brown eyes twinkle.

"I am completely and totally bejeezus-free," I confirm, trying and failing to be huffy and indignant. I narrow my eyes at him. "So what gives, then? You checking out the competition?" I grab at my sign-up sheet and flip it upside down defensively. "No trespassing."

A flush creeps up Theo's neck. "Actually," he says. "I wanted to ask you something."

For some reason, I feel fluttery and nervous. But what could Theo possibly want? I mean, he's Logan's running mate. He's not going to sign up for my carnival. Is he going to ask me to drop out of the race? "Yeah?"

He comes around to my side of the table and pulls

up a folding chair from against the wall. In one swift movement, he unfolds it and sits down next to me.

"You don't have a running mate," he says, stating the obvious rather baldly.

"I do," I insist. "She's just imaginary." I like to believe that the ghost of Edwina St. Claire is with me on this incredibly unexpected journey, but that's a secret that I'll take to my own grave.

It's not even a funny joke, but he does me the courtesy of coughing up a chuckle. Then his smile fades and he starts to look twitchy again.

"I know someone who might be less . . . invisible," he suggests slowly.

A strange feeling settles over me, like tiny little pinpricks all across the surface of my skin. I feel like I know what he's going to ask me, but then, at the same time, it doesn't make any sense at all. I raise an eyebrow at him questioningly.

"At your service?" he asks, looking about three years old and very hesitant.

Even with my electric currents of pre-knowing, it's still shocking. I am speechless for a beat, then remind myself to close my mouth. "You want to be my running mate?" The words sound ridiculous as they come out of my mouth.

"If you'll have me."

"Uh . . ." I have no idea what to say. Truly, none. I am devoid of words. It's not that I wouldn't "have him," so to speak. Theo is awesome. He's been a great VP for the past two years.

But he's been *Logan's* VP.

Almost involuntarily, I glance at Logan's table. Of course Theo notices.

"We already talked about it. It's cool."

"Really?" I'm dubious.

"Well, okay, not *cool*, so much as something we're going to deal with. I mean, I want to run with you. It's a done deal. Logan and I are 'broken up.'"

"So are we," I say shortly. Thankfully, Theo wisely doesn't reply to this non-news.

I compose myself, run my fingers thoughtfully through the tips of my ponytail. Do I feel weird about running with Theo?

Yeah, I do. It *is* weird. There's no getting around it.

But then again, it's not like people are banging down my door to help me out. And I well know that campaigns are hard work. Theo's a known quantity. He's a good guy.

"Am I allowed to ask what happened? The personal reasons?" Not to be overly nosy, but I'm absolutely crawling out of my skin with curiosity. Logan and Theo were practically the peanut butter and jelly of PHS student council. Or, if Logan and I were the pb&j, then Theo was a glass of skim milk. This split is bound to have a ripple effect.

"I want to save Everett Field," Theo says firmly. "Paige does, too." He smiles. "You're not the only fan of *Restless Nature*. There's a reason she goes by By_the_book."

By_the_book. Of course! "Anyway," he continues, "You're our best shot at doing that. Saving the field, I mean."

"Why?" I blurt, as though the concept is completely unfathomable. As though I'm not building my entire campaign on that whole theory.

He shrugs. "I have my reasons." He doesn't say more.

I nod, still letting the bizarreness of this situation wash over me like a bubble bath. After a moment, another thought occurs to me.

"What's Logan going to do?" I ask. "Without you?"

Theo tilts his head in the direction of Logan's table, where my ex-cutie (that's a technical term, of course) is barely visible behind a sea of starstruck worshippers. I'm appalled, but not entirely surprised, to see Shelby and Zoë included in the throng.

Shelby turns and makes eye contact with me for a moment. But only for a moment. Then Zoë whispers something to her, and she giggles, turning back to Logan and his entourage.

Theo turns back to me. "Think it over," he says. "For a day or two. I'm not going anywhere. But do not worry for one second about Logan." He sighs, mostly to himself. "Logan is going to be just fine."

☆ ☆ ☆ ☆ ☆

After school, Theo often stays behind to shoot some hoops with a few other guys from the varsity second string. As I approach him on the blacktop, the hollow rubbery thud of the basketball being dribbled echoes like my own heartbeat in my ears.

Theo races down the court, stopping short and leaping gracefully into a layup. The ball hits the rim, bounces out of bounds. He turns to retrieve it and sees me.

"Erin." He smiles. His face is sweaty and his cheeks are red. But he's definitely glad to see me.

☆ ☆ ☆ ☆ ☆

"We need to get the dirt on Caswell Corp."

I nod at Theo. "Good call."

I spent about four whole hours debating whether

105

or not to take Theo on as a running mate. Once you took the weirdness factor out of the equation — which was actually easier to do than I expected — it was kind of a no-brainer. And not that I'd ever admit it out loud, but I think there was a tiny, secret part of me that didn't mind sticking it to Logan a little bit. I was still so angry and hurt about our breakup that I felt like I deserved to have Theo on my side.

Besides, Theo says he has his reasons for not wanting to run with Logan. Personal reasons that I am not at all a part of. So obviously circumstances larger than both of us are at work here. Clearly.

Somewhat predictably, given that it was his big idea in the first place, Theo was thrilled with my decision, and suggested that we head to my place immediately after school to dive right into our planning. Which is where we are now, less campaigning than chewing on leftover pizza crusts with Paige, who swears she's in it for the guts, not the glory. Thank goodness. I don't know how much glory there is to be had by hanging around yours truly these days. Ever since Logan and I broke up, I think the popular vote might be stacked against me.

Paige shoves aside her paper plate and leans her elbows on the kitchen table. "I bet a group like Caswell has *great* dirt."

"Filth," Theo says. He's pacing the room, pausing periodically to peer at various clippings stuck on our fridge door.

"When's this from?" He points at one newspaper article.

"Oh, that was my father's first televised interview," I answer, not even really having to look up and see which one exactly he's pointing at.

"Right." Theo nods, making his floppy hair flop in sympathy. "Logan told me all about that night. Didn't your dad pop a bottle of champagne —" He cuts off abruptly, realizing that maybe I'm not up for the memory lane thing.

"Yup," I say quickly. "It was a fun night."

For a moment, we're all quiet.

"So, Caswell," Paige says, blessedly breaking the silence. "Dirty."

I shrug. "I don't know," I say. "I bet they're the type of group that keeps their noses pretty clean." The thing is, the big ones can usually pay for some industrial-strength Kleenex.

"We won't know until we Google," Theo rightly asserts, reaching across the table and grasping at my MacBook Air. He swings it around so that he's facing the screen and types in a quick string of words, smacking on the return key emphatically.

After a moment and a few more cautious taps, his eyes move across the screen, scanning intently. He mutters as he reads select phrases aloud. *"Third-largest development company in Illinois . . . growth of forty-two percent since two thousand and five . . . first became involved in local community* — oh." He stops abruptly, looking away from the computer.

"What, 'oh'?" Paige demands, scrambling over his shoulder to see for herself. Her eyes flicker as they take in the words. "Oh."

These "ohs" are sounding more and more ominous. I'm starting to get suspicious. "Show me," I say, my voice low.

Paige runs her fingers through her short, sleek platinum bob, looking concerned. "Promise not to freak?"

"Swear," I say automatically, crossing my fingers quickly behind my back. Paige doesn't know me well enough to know that I'd never make a promise like that. "Hit me."

Theo clears his throat and leans back in his chair, squinting at the computer screen. "The Caswell Corporation" — he pronounces every single syllable of the word — "first became involved in local community politics two months ago, when it decided to contribute a percentage of its annual profits to the campaign of current Plainsboro mayor running for re-election . . ."

108

He doesn't bother to finish the sentence. He doesn't need to.

The bowling ball is back, and this time it's made of lead. I want to curl up on the floor and close my eyes. With any luck, I'll wake up to find that Caswell Corp., breaking up with Logan, and the sale of Everett Field were only a dream.

Ha.

I take a deep breath and finish the sentence for Theo.

"Mayoral hopeful Caleb Bright."

Of course.

Fate's a funny thing, I guess.

Or maybe it's not fate. Maybe it's karma, or
kismet, or some other k-word that basically boils
down to the cosmos having a big old party at my
expense. I don't know. I'm not sure I even believe
in those k-words, anyway.

But I'll tell you what I do believe in: a big, fat
catch-22.

Literary references aside, a catch-22, of course,
is a darned-if-you-do, darned-if-you-don't sort of
scenario. The type of scenario with which I've
become all too familiar as of late.

Or, if you want to fall back onto the whole
freshman English template, I'm reminded of the short
story featuring the lady and the tiger. The details are

110

fuzzy now that I'm a world-weary upperclasswoman, but the gist is thus: A princessy type is told that if she wants to save her second-string, commoner beau, she must chose one of two outcomes for him.

Said studlycakes enters a corridor and faces two doors. Behind one is a beautiful lady. Behind the other is a deadly (not to mention, hungry) tiger. He doesn't know what's behind which door, but Her Highness does. The kicker is that *she* has to tell him which door to choose.

So either the princess sends her true love off to live happily ever after *with someone else,* or, basically, she sends him . . . off. And away from this mortal coil.

The author, lord bless his heart, never does tell us what our stalwart heroine chooses. It's more of a "What would you do?" kind of thing. Supposed to make you Think.

And I can tell you right now: I never did have any idea. And I sure as shish kebab don't have a clue now.

The lady or the tiger. My father or my field.

Dad's not going to be too pleased if I run my whole platform as a protest of his primary financiers.

But if I don't go up against Caswell Corp., Everett Field is essentially gone.

Once upon a time, this is the sort of thing I would have gone to Logan for. He was always good with the advice. Sigh.

Think now. What would you do?

It's not a rhetorical question, people. I could use a little help here. And soon. The countdown to election day – for Dad, and for me – is on.

Comments (1)

TeddyB: Tough call. But i think u know where i stand on the subject of rockin' the boat. Or should I say, "the *vote*." Hardy har har.

☆ Chapter Eight

I sleep fitfully, and when I wake, I feel like the insides of my eyelids have been coated in sandpaper. Beautiful.

I shrug myself into a well-cut pair of jeans and a button-down shirt, throwing a light wool sweater over my shoulders. I spend a few extra minutes shadowing and lining my eyes in the hopes of faking a few more hours of sleep. It doesn't really work, so I put on my glasses.

Downstairs, Mom pours herself a cup of coffee and Dad is settled at the kitchen table behind a huge hunk of the morning paper.

"How'd you sleep, sweetie?" Mom asks. *She*, of course, is perfectly polished in First Lady dress-down: a pair of deep indigo jeans, a black button-down shirt, and a kelly green wool blazer. Flawless as usual.

She looks up from the mug she's been stirring and takes me in. "Ah."

Ah. Not really a compliment.

"Yeah," I say, helping myself to a hearty dose of caffeine. "I'm pretty out of it." I dump a scoop of sugar the size of a small mountain into my coffee cup and swig, grimacing.

"Do you have time for breakfast?" Mom asks. When I get stressed out, I lose my appetite, and I can tell that she's noticed that lately, I've been wearing my belt one or two notches tighter. Unacceptable. I need to be healthy and robust for Dad's press appearances.

Dad. Press. Caswell Corp.

Everett Field.

Blagh.

I want to say something to him, but I have no idea what. I can't believe he's connected to Caswell. My dad — he of the Prius sedan, the man who took me to see *An Inconvenient Truth* in sneak previews! My fingertips quiver like live wires. Instead, I disappear back into my coffee, glancing distractedly at my watch. "Nothing to eat, thanks. I'm really late." I take one final gulp of coffee and deposit the mug in the sink. "I have to run."

Dad finally looks up from his paper, snapping at it so that it rustles loudly, making me flinch. "Erin — be home at six tonight. We're going to have a family meeting."

If there were a time to get it together to say something to him, that time would be now. I've got his attention.

I open my mouth, cough briefly, then clear my throat. Then I close my mouth again, push my chair back from the table, and gather my things.

Chicken.

"Sure," I say, calling to him over my shoulder.

Family meetings are a pretty common occurrence for the Bright household, but right now, I can't concentrate on that. I'm too preoccupied to even wonder what it is that my father wants to talk about.

Whatever it is, I'll find out later. For now, I just need to figure out a way to get through the day.

☆ ☆ ☆ ☆ ☆

Shelby hunts me down by my locker before the first bell rings. I've hit the Dunkin' Donuts drive-through, so I'm buzzing slightly from an extra shot of java when she stomps to a halt just in front of me.

"Hi," I say, blinking rapidly. I can't help it. I think I might be having an allergic reaction to the amount of coffee I've consumed.

115

"Morning." She raises her eyebrow at me meaningfully.

I'm not sure what it is she means to tell me, though.

"What's . . . up?" I ask cautiously.

I'm dying to tell her about my father and Caswell Corp., to run home together after school and hash it out over DIY manicures and a good skim through back issues of *Life and Style*, like the old days. Two weeks ago. But something tells me too much has happened for us to really go back to that now.

"Have you seen today's paper?" She looks equal parts horrified, pitying, and sympathetic. None of that can be good news.

"The *Ledger*? No, my dad was reading it this morning and I was late." Besides, it's not like we have a current events report due today or anything.

She sighs. Now her look is pure pity. I think I preferred her the other way, when she was slightly more inscrutable. "*The Slate.*" She rummages in the front pocket of her cargo skirt. "Zoë was the one who saw it. She said Allie called her and told her about it. I clipped the article for you." She shakes her head in defeat. "It was on the front page."

Whatever *it* is, it can't be good.

She passes the clipping to me, and all at once, I feel

dizzy. The newsprint swims in front of my eyes, and not because it's smudged.

I *wish* it were smudged, though. If it were smudged, I could avoid reading it. Avoid learning that some eagle-eyed reporter who clearly spends *way* too much time trawling the blogosphere found my post from last night. And decided to print it. Verbatim. And expose my entire crisis of conscience vis-à-vis my dad and Caswell Corp.

I curse those midnight press deadlines silently.

Shelby exhales loudly. "Sorry, Erin."

I nod in sheer disbelief. "Yeah." Me, too.

FIRST DAUGHTER TO CHOOSE DOOR NUMBER 2?
ERIN BRIGHT DENOUNCES CASWELL CORP — AND
DAD'S CAMPAIGN — ON PERSONAL BLOG.

God, those letters are so big and *bold*. Are all headlines so bold? Surely this required some sort of special printing technique.

"I told you not to get involved with all of this," Shelby reminds me. "Back when you first started freaking about Everett Field."

I look her straight in the eyes. "Yeah, you did," I say simply. She told me, warned me, and then she bailed on me.

117

I keep that part to myself.

I mean, she's working on Logan's campaign these days. I appreciate her heads-up — it means that we're not completely and totally strangers to each other — but still. There's not a whole lot left to say.

"Has your dad seen it yet?" she asks finally, knowing, as always, exactly what I'm thinking.

I shake my head shortly. "I don't think so."

Thank goodness for small favors, right?

Though somehow, I'm quite certain it's only a matter of time.

FROM: deathbycommittee@freenet.com
TO: firstgirlbright@blogorama.com
RE: Girl, please

When did you become all Reese Witherspoon in *Election*? You may be the mayor's daughter, but I remember back when the only debates you got involved in were frozen yogurt vs. sorbet, or flat iron vs. Japanese straightening treatment.

I liked you better then. And judging from the fact that you and Logan are splitsville, I'm not the only one.

Stick with lip gloss and low-fat licorice, Erin. It's what you know.

Plainsboro High is not a school lacking in pride or spirit. Lest anyone think that we students are all work and no play, this afternoon we've got a huge pep rally scheduled. I confess that I'm not at all above watching the football team bump chests while the cheerleaders spell words at top volume.

Zoë, Shelby, and I used to always go to these things together, but today, I don't even bother to seek them out beforehand. I think I've absorbed my quota of bad news and worse vibes for the afternoon as it is.

I think that watching the Plainsboro Roadrunners (no, really) run plays across the football field while pretty, athletic girls dance along to the Pussycat Dolls will make me smile. But about ten minutes into the rally, it becomes painfully obvious to me that, alas, I think wrong.

"You look like your puppy just died," Theo says, sidling up next to me offside.

I grin, realizing as I do that it's the first time I've smiled all day. "Not my puppy. Just my social life, my relationship, and, soon enough, my father's love for me."

"Right, just that," he says, wincing. He punches me lightly on the arm in a big-brother sort of way. "I saw the blog."

"You *commented* on the blog," I remind him. "You encouraged me to buck the system. And, by extension, my father. You're a bucker." Buckers are not particularly helpful in this situation.

"I have, on occasion, been known to stir up trouble," he admits. "But never deliberately." He looks thoughtful. "What did your father say? Was he furious? Did you guys talk about it?"

"Negative." I brighten, having an idea. "Hey," I say, grabbing him by his own forearm. "*You* should be the one to deal with my father."

Because I can't. I swear, I'd run away and join the circus, if only it were a more practical solution. But I'm really not sure about those big shoes the clowns have to wear. Clowns are kind of scary.

"Forget your parents. And your friends. Your *other* friends," he corrects himself. "Forget Logan."

"Good plan," I say. "Any idea how to go about that?"

"As a matter of fact," he says, his chocolate-brown eyes twinkling, "yes. There's a Judd Apatow festival playing downtown. It starts at five. Three movies, three chances to see people pratfall through various raunchy premises only to discover in the final act that they do, in fact, have a heart."

"I do love Seth Rogan," I say, considering. "*Superbad*?"

"Is the first up," he confirms, glancing at his watch. "Are you in? Have you got anything else going on?"

With the exception of Theo, Paige, and Mindy, I'm not exactly prom queen these days. I think my dance card is pretty well free.

"Nothing," I say, warming to the idea of eating my way out of a huge tub of popcorn and gorging on obscene quantities of peanut M&M's. My mother does *not* approve of peanut M&M's. But my mother and her impeccably pressed blazer won't be at the movies. . . .

I link my arm through Theo's. "Let's do it."

Seth Rogan's problems have got to be more entertaining than my own, right?

☆ *Chapter Nine*

"I think that Judd Apatow might be on to something," Theo says, leading me through the multiplex parking lot and back to my car.

"He does have a firm grasp on comedic timing," I agree, nodding and taking a slurp from my oversize cup of soda. "If only he'd do a movie about a high school election. That would really hit me where I live." Like a knife to the heart maybe. Fun.

"Well, there's *Election,* but it's not Judd Apatow and it probably wouldn't do much for your mood," Theo says.

"Right, my mood." It's hard to believe, but I'd actually forgotten my mood for a few hours. Movies really are magic. "It's improving, I think."

"Good." We reach my car, and Theo stops just between me and the driver's side door. "I don't like seeing you down."

Obviously, I don't especially like *being* down, either. But for some reason, his concern feels very . . . *specific* to me right now.

And then suddenly, something changes. I can't exactly explain it, but my cheeks feel warm, my fingertips are tingly, and my heart thumps against my rib cage. At first, I'm not sure what's going on, and then it dawns on me — I'm nervous. Theo's concern is making me nervous. Because I've just realized what it is that Theo's concern feels like.

It feels like crushing. Like concern with a capital L-U-R-V-E.

But that would be crazy. No — that would be *insane*. Theo couldn't possibly be digging on me in that way. I mean, I'm Logan's ex. Logan's very recent ex. Maybe on another planet, or another time . . .

I know Theo said that he and Logan "broke up" as running mates because of the whole Everett Field thing. But somehow I doubt the Guy Code allows him to make a play for me now.

Not that Theo isn't adorable, it's just — he's *Theo*. And I'm *Erin*. And as much as we've put the whole awkwardness behind us so that he can run my campaign with me, any romantic sort of . . . *concern* would just be taking things to a whole different level of bizarro.

123

"So," Theo says softly, breaking into my thoughts. He steps forward.

I step backward. "So," I repeat. How can I diffuse this situation without making things even weirder, or, worse, accidentally insulting Theo? Boys' egos are very fragile. I have firsthand knowledge of this fact.

"Where did you park, again?" I blurt. It's inspired, non sequitur or no. We'd taken separate cars to school, so we drove separately to the movies. Phew. That reduces our uncomfortably-ambiguous-encounter quotient by a marginal percent. It's a small victory, but I'll take it.

"Oh." Theo stops in his tracks suddenly, looking confused. "Um . . ." He glances out toward the expanse of the lot, scanning it. He points. "There."

He could be pointing at the Goodyear Blimp, for all that it matters to me.

"Right," I say. I step forward tentatively, then screw up my confidence, square my shoulders, and decide to take control of the situation. "Right." I give him a strictly platonic one-armed hug. That sends a message, right? One-armed hugs, in my opinion, score significantly lower on the lurve-o-meter.

"Thanks again," I say warmly, in a tone that I hope conveys sincerity but not uncertainty. It was, after all, a *firm* one-armed hug. "I really needed that." I rummage in my coat pocket, dig out my car keys, and push the button on my key chain that makes the little *bloop* sound that means the doors are now unlocked. "I've got to get home. My dad —"

And then I stop. And remember.

That I really *have* got to get home.

Like, pronto. Because more than twelve hours ago, my father called a family meeting for this evening. And all at once, I have a good idea of what it is that he wants to talk about.

I can't think of the last time that I flaked out on my parents or on a family meeting. I am in so, so, so much trouble. Grounded-until-I'm-thirty sort of trouble.

"Your dad," Theo repeats. "Do you have plans with him?"

I nod, my heart sinking.

My funk is back. With reinforcements in the form of major stress. If I thought things couldn't possibly get more complicated, I obviously was very, very wrong.

☆ ☆ ☆ ☆ ☆

My parents are not the sort to pace back and forth frantically, peering out the window every four seconds or so, issuing high-octane AMBER alerts when I break curfew.

This mainly has to do with the fact that the first and last time I broke curfew, ever, was on the morning I was born, when I arrived three days after my mother's doctor had predicted.

No, on the whole, I'm the boringly punctual, responsible type. Which means that my parents have had to work hard concocting alternative means of displaying their displeasure with my behavior, on the rare occasion that the situation calls for such.

Today is one of those rare occasions. I open the front door to our house with dread, and am surprised to find, after stumbling tentatively inside, utter silence. No wailing mother, no high-pitched ringing of phones, no father shouting angrily or banging his fists on the table.

Nothing.

"Hello?" I call.

Nothing.

I venture farther into the house, winding my way through the foyer, past the living room and kitchen, and into the office. My father, at least, can usually be found in the office. When he's not, you know, in his actual office.

Bingo. I've stumbled into an alternate reality where my father and mother have been replaced by robots. Extremely even-tempered, placid, docile robots.

My mother sits at her little desk, humming quietly to herself. She has a sterling silver letter opener in her hand and is slicing through envelopes rhythmically, almost in time to her humming. She's found a headband that exactly matches her blazer, making her seem even more like a life-size Barbie doll. My father is sitting back in his designer leather recliner, skimming something affixed to a clipboard.

I clear my throat. My mother looks up, placing her letter opener down on the surface of her desk. "Erin. We didn't hear you come in." Her tone is impossible to analyze.

"Yeah, I . . . well, I went to the movies," I admit. "I had kind of a weird day at school, and I was looking to take my mind off of . . . stuff."

"What a coincidence," my father says, rising up out of his chair and placing his clipboard aside on an end table. "*We* had an interesting day, too." His eyes have turned the color of the ocean before a storm, a possible sign of imminent freak-outage. My father's not the type to shout and scream, but this complete composure? Totally freaky.

I decide to preempt them, go nuts with the hand-wringing and apologizing. Beat 'em at their own game, you know?

"I'm sorry." I jump right in with both feet. "I really

didn't mean to miss the family meeting. Especially since . . ." I wince. "I'm pretty sure I know what you wanted to talk about."

Dad raises an eyebrow at me. It's sarcasm. Caleb Bright has resorted to sarcasm. This is not good.

"Really? Say more."

"Say more" is classic Caleb Bright. It's a rhetorical tactic that usually manipulates his opponent into revealing too much and proverbially hanging him- or herself.

"The . . . blog?" I venture.

I'm doing that thing where I end statements in a question. Normally it drives my mom crazy. Today, however, I have already driven her thirteen kinds of insane, so she is not about to quibble over the smaller details.

"The blog!" she says, managing to sound equal parts deranged and delighted. "Yes."

"I wasn't thinking," I offer.

"Obviously," Mom says. "This morning, we saw the blog in the paper — always the ideal way to learn about one's daughter's doings: the newspaper, the Internet — and we were hoping to talk to you about it tonight. Specifically with regard to the damage that you could be doing to your father's campaign if you keep up with this rash of honesty that seems to have you in its bony clutches."

And here I always thought honesty was a good policy. The best, even. But I can see where she's coming from.

"Still," my father continues, taking the conversational reins firmly in hand. "We've moved beyond that."

"That's . . . good," I say cautiously, pretty sure it's really not all that good.

"No, there's a new concern on the horizon," he says, sounding mildly bewildered.

I think back to Theo's concern, over at the movie theater, outside of my car, and I realize that over the course of today, concern has taken on a decidedly negative connotation. I could probably do with fewer concerns in my life right about now.

Nevertheless, I rally. Now's the time for rallying, I feel. "Say more," I reply brightly, then immediately regret it. I hope Dad doesn't think I'm teasing him. Teasing would be a very bad call just now.

Luckily, my father is too preoccupied with his concern to worry about being teased. "About an hour ago," he says, rubbing at his chin, "I got a phone call."

Seeing as how phone calls are not that eventful, I

decide there must be more to this anecdote and sit tight, silent.

"It was Channel Three," he goes on.

Channel Three is a local cable access station. It runs on technology only slightly more sophisticated than a telephone made of aluminum cans and string, but everyone in Plainsboro watches it. It has all of the exclusive mayoral campaign interviews and election coverage.

"What did they want?"

"They want to interview you," my mother chimes in. Thankfully, she has stepped very far away from the letter opener, which bears too close a resemblance to a deadly weapon for my liking.

"They want to interview you? That's great!" I smile at my father, willing him psychically to return the grin.

Yeah. I am not psychic.

"No, Erin," he says, bearing down on me with the full force of his stately six feet, two inches of height. "They don't want to interview 'you'" — he points to himself. "They want" — now he waves his hand back and forth between us, like he's trying to shift the ions in the air — "to interview 'you.' Collective 'you.'"

I get it. "*Us* 'you'?"

He nods. "Us you. They want us to go head-to-head. To debate. About the blog and Caswell Corporation."

My eyes widen and my lungs collapse in on me. I'd say I can't believe this is happening to me, but since I can't believe *most* of what's been happening to me lately, I think it might be time to start rethinking my suspension of disbelief.

"What . . . what did you tell them?" I ask, horrified.

Now he smiles. "What do you think?"

TOP FIVE REASONS TO APPEAR ON
LOCAL TELEVISION WITH MY FATHER*
*(note: http.firstgirlbright.blogorama.com is on temporary hiatus. I will be writing longhand until such a time as the security features of my blog have been upgraded (say, from "nonexistent," to "nominally existent"). No sense taking chances. If you are reading this journal, this is your LAST CHANCE to turn back before completely violating my freedom of privacy. Or whatever. Just back away from the diary slowly, bucko, and no one will get hurt.)

5) Give Dad a chance to save some face after the debacle with the paper and my

blog post, show people that he's got his daughter under control.

Potential downside: Much as I want to help Dad, I'm not sure "under control" is such a compliment or good thing to be.

4) Explain my point of view.

Potential downside: So far, my point of view hasn't exactly been met with wild enthusiasm (Theo aside, that is. And that was a problem for other reasons).

3) Experience my notorious fifteen minutes of fame.

Potential downside: It's local television, not HBO On Demand. Also, television lighting does icky things to my skin.

2) Provides opportunity to make on-air "grand gesture" to Logan and possibly rekindle our relationship.

Potential downside: Humiliation, rejection. Also, Logan's been kind of a jerk lately.

1) According to Dad, he's already agreed to do it — for the both of us. So really, there's no turning back now.

Potential downside: Agh.

☆ *Chapter Ten*

"Babydoll. If you don't hold still, you're going to end up with Cleopatra eyes."

Frannie gently coaxes my head upward by the tip of my chin. She grabs an airbrusher gun off the kitchen table, brandishing it threateningly.

I flinch. "Is that necessary? I mean, it's Channel Three."

Frannie frowns at me. "Are you joking?"

I'm not joking. But neither is she. There's a reason that Dad and Mom brought hair and makeup in for a house call at the crack of oh-my-jeez.

Next to Frannie, Mena taps her foot restlessly. She slaps a straightening iron into her palm. The sound of the metal against her skin is soothing. "And meanwhile," she says wryly, "I'm here to jump in for your round two."

Frannie digs into an oversize fisherman's tackle box

that spills over with glitter, shadows, powders, liners, and big, fluffy brushes. "You're going to have to wait your turn," she tells Mena, with a crooked grin that exposes her adorable two front buckteeth.

She plucks two different tubes of mascara out of the box. "Demure," she says, thrusting a browny-gray one at me. "And audacious." Audacious is a heavier black.

She drums her fingers against the tablecloth. I notice that her fingernails are chipped and uneven. I guess makeup artists are more concerned with other people's appearances than their own.

She breathes in, seeming to come to a decision. "I think . . . audacious." She winks at me. "Are you feeling audacious today?"

☆ ☆ ☆ ☆ ☆

Audacity may be the last thing I'm feeling right now, but I'm certain Dad thinks I've got it in spades. Our ride over to the studio feels suffocating and cramped, even though we've each got a quadrant of stretch limo all to ourselves.

Dad shuffles some note cards in his lap while Mom quietly files away at a perfectly even, perfectly shaped pinky nail. No one looks at me or says anything.

I clear my throat. But not audaciously.

☆ ☆ ☆ ☆ ☆

Channel Three may not be *Dateline*, but that doesn't mean I'm not freaking out.

In fact, I think I may have passed "freaking out" about an hour or two ago. Now I'm careening toward "losing it completely," with no hope of getting it back together in sight.

I feel like a nest of live wires is tangled up in my stomach. I wonder if this is what people feel like after they've been struck by lightning.

Of course, this is no big deal for Dad. He's done Channel Three a zillion times. That's why he's perched in his oversize director's chair looking as though it's a La-Z-Boy. He could fall asleep, he's just that comfortable, clutching at an oversize coffee mug that I'm pretty sure only holds water.

The studio itself is small and bare-bones. Mom hovers off to one side, looking thin and tired, but excited. A few harried assistant-types wander back and forth carrying clipboards. Nothing about this is very glamorous. And yet I still feel a little bit like a movie star. Though I've been on TV and in the news a bunch of times with Dad, it was always "*with* Dad," as in, total accessory, not saying anything, no one caring about me except to notice that my skirt wasn't accidentally tucked into my panty hose and I wasn't picking my nose in public.

I subtly tug at the hem of my skirt, smoothing it out. I'm not wearing panty hose today, but better safe than sorry.

My suede top-handled tote buzzes in my lap, alerting me of a new text message.

Logan used to text me all sorts of goofy messages whenever I was doing public appearances with Dad. We had a bet going: He was trying to get me to crack, smile, laugh, or otherwise break character in the middle of one of these things. He never succeeded, but he came pretty close. A text from Logan would really help right now.

I fish my phone out of my purse and flip it open.

KNOCK 'EM DEAD, FIRST DAUGHTER – T

Not Logan. Theo.

Still, it's a sweet gesture. Thoughtful.

But it's not Logan.

"Cell phones off."

A thick cloud of Estee Lauder Beautiful and Sebastian Spray Gel announces Alisha Owens, Channel Three's main talking head. She looks like she had about five Frannies working on her. Since five A.M. today. In a good way.

She smiles, her eyes lighting up. "Are you ready?"

136

☆ ☆ ☆ ☆ ☆

I sit next to my father, facing out at the cameras. No studio audience for us. My legs are crossed demurely at the ankle, as dictated to me by Alisha Owens. She explained to me about skirts and the basic principles of modesty. Thank goodness. Otherwise I would have totally crossed at the knees, and *then* who knows? Crisis averted.

"Everybody ready?" Alisha asks brightly, sitting in her own director's chair on the opposite side of my father. We're all miked in and ready to go. We nod, and I swallow hard.

A woolly-haired PA standing by my mother holds his fingers out as he counts down: "In five . . . four . . . three . . . two . . ."

"I'm Alisha Owens," Alisha says, jumping in smoothly and giving a toothy white grin. "And I'm here today with Mayor Caleb Bright, who, as I'm sure you all know, is currently running for a second term. With us, too, is Caleb's daughter, Erin, a junior at Plainsboro High School."

We both flash a smile at the camera. I furtively hope that I don't have any Lancôme Juicy Tube on my teeth. There's no way to check. I cross my fingers discreetly in my lap and try to run my tongue across my front teeth in a way that won't make my lips pooch out conspicuously.

"Sixteen-year-old Erin is running for Plainsboro student council president. One of the primary issues of her campaign is the need to raise money for a new school arts program, which in turn would poten- tially negate the need for the Board of Education to move forward with its sale of historic site Everett Field to local development heavyweight the Caswell Corporation."

When she puts it that way, I sound kind of noble, almost. And doomed.

"Is that correct, Erin?"

What? Of course it's correct. We went over these questions in the green room. Which was more like a green broom closet, but that's not the point. The point is that she knows that it's correct.

Back to reality, Erin. This may be cable access, but it's still live.

I nod slightly, not wanting to muss my carefully placed low ponytail. "Yes, it is."

I am rocking Channel Three.

"And, this is rather ironic, because the Caswell Corporation is one of the major funders of your father's campaign, correct?"

Also correct. And awkward. "Yes," I say shortly. "Which I didn't realize when I first set out to try to save the field."

"Of course not," Alisha agrees. I can see how she got this job. She's supersympathetic. I want to talk to her about all of this stuff for hours, just so that she can tell me that she gets it and that I'm not an awful person. She also seems to know a bit about eyebrow pencils, which could come in handy sometime.

"Can you tell us a little bit more about why the field is such an important place to you?" Alisha prods. Again, she knows I can. But I guess this is her "natural lead-in" style.

I'm about to open my mouth and speak — I've got the answer all mapped out, remember, from our pre-show prep — when it hits me: I've never really told anyone (other than Logan, that is) about my dream of becoming a writer. And now I'm about to spill it on live television. Mind you, there may only be, like, thirteen or so people watching this show right now, but still. This is kind of big.

I take a deep breath and go for it. "Well, as most people know, Everett Field was the location where Plainsboro's own Edwina St. Claire wrote *Restless Nature,* her essay collection."

Alisha widens her eyes in a very "mmm-hmm" sort of manner. It's encouraging, so I warm to my story.

"What a lot of people — even my friends — don't know is, Edwina St. Claire is my favorite writer and also my heroine. She was one of the most influential female writers of the late nineteenth century, and I've read *Restless Nature* dozens of times. Some of you may be familiar with my blog" — here I offer a rueful laugh at my own expense, *oh, ha-ha, my public humiliation is a source of constant amusement* — "which, though it seems to have taken on a life of its own, was started as a modern-day version of the type of journaling that Edwina St. Claire made her life — and her career — from."

I glance at Dad. He looks surprised. Not in any way that anyone else in the world would notice, mind you. But there's a slight twitch in the lower left corner of his mouth that tells me he's listening to me.

Alisha looks thoughtful. "So you're interested in becoming a writer?"

I nod. "Yes," I say quietly, feeling suddenly shy. "And the field has a lot of meaning for me."

Now that I've come clean, admitted my wildest dreams and goals aloud, I'm feeling bolder, more confident. I sit up straighter and brush my bangs out of my eyes.

"But the truth is, I honestly believe that Everett Field should have meaning for all of us here in Plainsboro. It's a historic site, yes, but it also represents an appreciation for nature and the environment. Don't we have enough gas stations in Plainsboro as it is? Aren't the giant SUV gas-guzzlers on our roads doing enough to harm our environment? What happened to going green? While I support the school board's efforts to raise money for the new arts program, I don't see why we should have to sacrifice the field in order to do so. That kind of feels like cutting off our nose to spite our face."

I pause, realizing that I've just experienced the verbal equivalent of a hemorrhage. I'm not sure how it's going to be received.

Alisha looks slightly numb, but my father's got a different glint in his eye. I thought he might want to strangle me after I admitted that whole "writing is my life's ambition" thing, but instead, he mostly looks . . . proud. Proud?

Huh. Go figure.

"And what was your reaction when you first found out about Caswell Corp.'s connection to your father's campaign?"

Oh, the hard questions. Bring 'em on.

"I basically wanted to puke," I say frankly. It works.

The handful of Channel Three employees standing around watching our taping chuckle. Even my father's mouth turns up at the corners ever-so-slightly.

"I can only imagine," Alisha replies, looking charmed by my chutzpah. "Of course, you know that Caswell has done a lot of great work in building up Plainsboro's economy."

"Oh, I know all of the statistics," I say. "My running mate and I researched it all when we first put together our campaign platform. And I don't blame my father for wanting to do business with them.

"I just hope he doesn't blame me for sticking to my guns."

I hazard another sidelong glance at my father. The corners of his mouth are in full twitch, and his eyes have returned to their Caribbean Sea shade. No more stormy weather ahead. The forecast is sunny and maybe even, if I'm lucky, bright (pun fully intended). He's going to run his campaign, and I'm going to run mine.

And we're both going to do it our own way. No compromises.

It's on. And I'm raring to go.

☆ ☆ ☆ ☆ ☆

Later, I feel like a balloon that someone has pricked with a safety pin. I lean back against the plush town car seats, clutching at a bottle of spring water. The moist plastic is cool to my touch. If I were any more inanimate, my body would actually fuse to the seat.

My parents, however, are ramrod straight as ever, like someone braced their spines with bamboo shoots. Mom swigs a Diet Coke like it's her job.

"Alisha didn't ask about your relationship with Logan," she says. "I'm surprised."

She sounds almost disappointed that I wasn't fully humiliated on live television.

"I spoke to her beforehand," Dad clarifies. "I told her it was off limits."

Oh.

He coughs. "You know, Erin, I was pleased with the way you handled yourself in there. It's obvious you're learning to stick to your principles."

"Thank you?" It sounds like a compliment. But I can't be sure.

"I do wish," he goes on, "that your principles were more in line with mine."

So there it is. We're okay, Dad and I. For now.

But only okay.

I know, I know. I said I was taking a break from the blogosphere until things cooled down a little bit.

Well, I lied.

The truth is, I realize now that I'm not looking for things to cool down. Nope. Rather, what I'd like would be to heat things up. In fact, I'd love it if we could all get going toward our collective boiling point.

Work with me:

I'm sure my father would prefer it if the main focus of my campaign weren't to bring down the company that supports his. He may not be superthrilled with what I had to say about Caswell. But Dad was totally down with how I composed

144

myself on Channel Three. He told me in so many words. And he was touched to hear how devoted I am to writing, and to the environment, and to Everett Field. So even though things aren't superperfect between us, now I have his blessing to go forth and raise money.

What I need, then, is you. *All* of you. Not your blessing – though that would definitely be all warm and fuzzy – but your actual physical person, and hopefully, some of your brain, too.

Consider this a call to arms.

We're going to save Everett Field. We're going to raise an arts fund. We are going to completely and totally rock out.

I can't do this without you.

Join me tomorrow, after school, for our first annual Bright Fund-raising Carnival!

Here's to bucking the party line – with a party! It must be done. And with any luck, we'll sway the popular vote while we're at it.

<u>Comments (1)</u>

DeathbyCommittee: ok, ok, so u're blogging about parties again. Yay, you. But why all the political leanings? It just ain't natural.

☆ Chapter Eleven

"Oh. My. God."

"*Erin.* It was a call to arms."

"I know. It's just, I wasn't expecting . . . quite so many . . . arms."

Or faces. When I banged out a few hundred words and sent them off into the blogosphere last night, I don't think I had any idea that people were actually listening.

Certainly not so *many* people, anyway.

They must have seen the posters.

The line for the carnival snakes all the way out of the high school gymnasium, down the hallway, along the front steps to the school, and outside, where it winds around the block. I catch tons of people I know — and even a bunch I don't — standing in line, looking enthusiastic.

I pop back into the gym, where my trusty volunteers are putting the finishing touches on their booths before we officially open our doors.

I turn to Theo. "Do we have a plan? For crowd control?"

He looks at me like I've sprouted an extra eye in the center of my forehead. "Erin, breathe," he commands. "You can do this. You were *born* to do this." He smiles. "Literally. It is your birthright." He grabs my shoulders firmly and pushes me toward the front of the throng.

And that's what it is, really — a throng. I mean, I've been to my dad's victory parties before. He would be pretty impressed by this throng.

After a few years of tagging along at my father's events, I've learned to eyeball a crowd. I'd say there are about sixty or seventy-five kids out here. Sixty may not sound like a lot, but you'd be surprised. There's strength in numbers. That's all politics really is, when you get down to it: strength in numbers.

Of course, my favorite number used to be a small one: two. Just me and Logan.

Logan *loves* carnivals. His favorite thing in the world is when the Strawberry Festival comes to Plainsboro in April. He's a whiz at Whac-A-Mole and has won me no fewer than three stuffed moles in our time together.

But something tells me he won't be here today.

I clamber toward the most frontlike section of the throng and wave. Instead of quieting down, though, my public (I have a public! Well, Everett Field does, anyway. Which is even better, of course. This is not about my ego, I have to remind myself) immediately begins to hoot, holler, and whistle. It's a good thing I'm not a blusher. Off in the corner, straining at my peripheral vision, Paige and Theo stomp their feet. Is this what my father feels like all the time?

Because I could get used to this.

Not about my ego. Right.

"Hi, guys," I call out tentatively.

Deafening cheers. I think I even hear a yodel in there, for good measure, though for all I know, that's Theo again. For some reason, he just seems like the type of guy who might toss a good-measure yodel into the mix every now and then.

I'm feeling bolder. Also, if I don't raise my voice, no one will be able to hear me. Crazy, right?

"We're all here because we want to save Everett Field, right?"

Shrieks, clapping. I take it all as an overwhelming yes.

"Well, my advisory committee"— I point toward Paige and Theo, who wave agreeably —"and I have

149

consulted extensively about what our best options are for raising money. And we've decided that our soundest strategy is to have an afternoon of FUN!"

For a moment, no one says or does anything. People seem very uncertain. I feel a twinge of doubt. Did I bomb? Is the chirping of crickets next?

Brilliantly, though, it's at this moment that Theo decides to act. He raises two fingers to his mouth and actually whistles the way they do in cartoons or movies. It's superloud and makes the shorter strands of my eyebrows stand on end. I didn't know they could do that.

It works, though. I take one more deep breath, surreptitiously do what I can about rogue eyebrow hairs, and then I'm bum-rushed. It's a freakin' stampede.

And it's really, really cool.

☆ ☆ ☆ ☆ ☆

At first I think my favorite thing about the carnival is popcorn-cart popcorn. And lemonade. But it quickly becomes clear that I'm equally enamored of cotton candy and fried dough.

I am *so* glad we solicited food donations from local restaurants.

I'm wolfing down my second cotton candy when I'm jostled from behind. "Watch it," I say, trying not to sound too annoyed as crystallized sugar adheres to my chin.

I whirl around. It's Logan.

His chin is decidedly sugarless, which instantly makes me feel foolish.

"You came," I blurt. Now I feel even more stupid. If only I were standing here in my underwear. Then I'd have achieved a complete trifecta of ridiculousness.

"Yeah, I brought Ian."

Ian is Logan's younger brother. He's eleven, and worships the ground Logan walks on. Logan adores Ian and is always doing stuff with him. Since I'm an only child, I totally got an extra kick out of spending time with Ian when Logan and I were still together.

I glance around. "Is he hiding?"

Logan laughs, then abruptly cuts off, as if he just remembered that we're not in love anymore. "Dunking booth."

"Awesome," I say. "Who's up now?"

"Mindy Jackson. Zoë and Allie just *dropped* her —" He cuts off again, possibly for different reasons this time.

"Right."

151

"I'd better go," he says, clutching at his own cotton candy.

And then he does. Leaving me feeling like it's my own heart that's been plunged into the icy-cold dunking tank and left there until it's completely waterlogged.

☆ ☆ ☆ ☆ ☆

"I'm still tallying." Theo states this with a flourish, brandishing a carrot stick dipped in hummus like a king's scepter.

"You might tally better if you quit with the snacking," Paige snarks cutely.

After school, Paige, Theo, and I retreated to Headquarters Central, aka my kitchen. Ever since my television appearance, Mom has been extra weird about my campaigny life, to the point that she's even downgraded the snacks she keeps stocked in the pantry. Where once there were pretzel sticks, we've got pitas, veggies, and the aforementioned hummus. All of which I'm dipping into quite enthusiastically at the moment. A girl's got to keep up her strength if she's going to save Everett Field, raise money for a school arts program, and triumph over student council elections all in the same week.

152

"Drumroll?" I prompt, causing Theo to play his carrot stick like he's auditioning for a band, while liberally spraying our tabletop with pureed chickpea.

"It's not . . . exactly what we expected," he warns. "Two hundred tickets, at five dollars a ticket . . ."

"A thousand dollars? That's all?"

I can't help it. I know that's great — any amount of money we raise is great — but it's not enough. A thousand dollars will barely buy illustration software for our school computers.

It made sense, anyway. "I guess we should have seen this coming."

"Maybe," Paige argues, "but the carnival was awesome. And it's still cash. The school board will appreciate cash. How could it not?" She tugs at the tips of her bob thoughtfully. "I was thinking we could have raised at least five thousand. Remind me never to start my own business."

Charity is charity, of course, and I was grateful that the carnival had been such a success. But my campaign — and our cause — were turning out to be kind of costly, and I had a feeling that we were about to find ourselves pretty darn disappointed.

With an educational discount, one new, fully loaded, brand-spankin'-new and up-to-date desktop with special art software would cost our school library five hundred tax-deductible dollars. I knew this. I had done the research. Ironically, I'd done it on my own (well, and Dad's and Mom's, but I like to think of it as my own) gorgeous, totally modernized home computer.

Fact: $1,000 still wasn't enough.

"We could buy . . . some easels, a scanner, and a can of paint, maybe," I moan, slumping over my kitchen table. The big push to save Everett Field? Was a big, fat bust. Maybe I'll just never eat again.

"But – it could be metallic paint. It's fancier," Paige chimes in helpfully. "Way fancier." She eyes me encouragingly.

This little tidbit has the effect of causing me to groan even more loudly. "It's hopeless. *I'm* hopeless."

"You are *not* hopeless," Theo insists, his chocolate-brown eyes glinting sternly. "You raised, like, a whole entire color scanner. It was your idea. All you!"

"Without a proper arts studio and program, what good will the scanner do?" I ask.

What did I tell you? Hopeless. Completely and utterly hopeless.

Theo flips the notebook open and starts skimming through it, running his index finger along the lines of the page. "I haven't told you the best part yet."

"There's another best part?" I ask, excited. "Better than the money?"

He arches a devilish eyebrow. "What would you say if I told you that I saw Zoë sacrifice at least twenty bucks to skeeball?"

I laugh. "She loves skeeball."

"Yeah, well, it doesn't love her. She lost three rounds. And twenty bucks."

I shrug. "Karma is a boomerang."

At least, I hope.

☆ ☆ ☆ ☆ ☆

If my life were a teen movie, this would be the part where the pop music kicks in and suddenly we're all traipsing through a montage of campaigny activities. You'd see me in my room, dressing in seventeen different perfectly color-coordinated outfits, only to finally settle on jeans, a hoodie, and my lavender Skechers because I want to seem like a woman of the people. Then there'd be me, stopping for a hearty shot of java with Theo and Paige on our way to the school parking lot, which is where my campaign volunteers meet up every morning.

Next would be me patting perky do-gooders like Missy Jackson on the back as they wrestle a stack of heavy, homemade posters into the passenger seat of their mother's SUV. Me suggesting Missy and Co.

somehow find room for an extra box of specially printed bumper stickers on the floor of the backseat. Me smiling patiently as I explain to Missy's wingman (winggirl?) that plastic shopping bags are not an acceptable, environmentally friendly means of toting materials to and from school.

It'd be a great montage. The music would be perfect, upbeat, peppy — suitable for *TRL* rotation — and the cuts would be lively, frenetic, and fun. Hilary Duff might play me, with Ashley Tisdale and Zac Efron starring as Paige and Theo, respectively. Good times.

Movie montage would totally kick butt.

Real-life, however, was a slightly different story.

http://firstgirlbright.blogorama.com
October 6, 6:11 pm

If there's one thing that I've learned from my father, it's that a good politician can spin just about anything. There's always a silver lining, a bright side, or just the plain old power of positive thinking. And usually that's enough. Usually.

I guess this is all by way of saying that – much as it pains me to admit this – I'm not all that great of a politician.

Don't get me wrong – I've got some good news.

Namely: Our carnival managed to raise a thousand dollars. And truly, that's more than just great. That's *amazing*. And that's all you.

Let's put those numbers into perspective, shall we? $1000 translates to roughly five hundred tubes of Paula Dorf lip tint in the shade of your choice.

Or nine hundred episodes of *The Hills* downloaded from iTunes. It's a few pairs of Levi's premium denim stonewashed jeans, and at least a year of manicure-pedicures at the mid-range salon of your choice. It's a year of Netflix, four pairs of custom Nikes, three at-home teeth whitening kits.

It's a lot of things. Things that, once upon a time, if not now, played a huge part in my day-to-day life (teeth-whitening strips in particular. Those things are *amazing*. Though they sometimes make your gums tingle).

But you know what it's not?

It's not enough money to save Everett Field.

I'd be lying if I said I wasn't disappointed. I'd rather see the field around for a jillion years to come, rather than a hideous gas station that pollutes the air and also the landscape. But it is not to be.

So there's the bad news, in plain black and white. There's not a whole lot that I can do to pretty it up for you, except to remind you again that while $1,000.00

may not be enough to save Everett Field, it is definitely something to be so, so proud of.

How's that for spin control?

<u>Comments (4)</u>

Sby16: Really, tho, E? U gave it your best shot.

TeddyB: You may be disappointed, but I say, *brava!* U've still got my vote.

Asoren: So confused. What do Nikes and Netflix have to do with our Everett Field? U politicians & ur double-talk.

By_the_book: How many tubes of lip tint do you go through in a year, anyway?

From: **Princelogan@freenet.com**
To: **Firstgirlbright@blogorama.com**

Ian wanted me to tell you that he had a blast at the carnival. So, thanks.
PS: $1,000 is kind of a lot of money, you know.

☆ *Chapter Twelve*

I've been so caught up in my own drama, with Everett Field and the election and everything else, that I almost forget that there's a whole other political campaign going on. Namely, my father's.

Obviously it'd be totally impossible to completely forget, especially because my father and mother haven't forgotten. Not if their semifrantic, worried, nails-bitten-to-the-quick pace around the house is any sort of indicator. With Caleb Bright, polls can only be counted on for so much. He needs numbers a mayor-elect could count on. He needs *ballots*.

Normally I'd be more involved in their stress sessions, but the truth is that things have been kind of strained since the Channel Three interview and the Caswell Corp. drama.

Dad may be proud of me for speaking my mind, but that doesn't mean things aren't awkward. The press still loves to make a whole thing — "father pitted against daughter! Drama! Intrigue!" — and the whole thing's got mom totally on edge. More than strained. Pureed.

I don't enjoy it.

I try to keep my own bad moodiness to myself, as much as I can. I really don't think moaning about how much I miss Logan, or how lousy a job I'm doing at saving Everett Field, is going to go over that well with them right now. I sort of worry that they'd tell me I asked for it.

And to tell you the truth, I sort of worry that they'd be right.

In the days immediately following the carnival, our house is a constant whirlwind. Dad has his office at town hall, of course, but his work follows him home. No, scratch that — his work follows him *everywhere*. He's like the Pied Piper of paperwork. Our fax machine constantly twitters like it's receiving messages from somewhere just outside of Pluto's orbit.

Meanwhile, Mom keeps herself busy by throwing herself full force into her own campaign for Wife of the Year. Here I always thought *my* grooming was impeccable, but Mom completely schools me in how it's done. Most mornings, she's up by 5 A.M. (insanity), at which point she hits the gym for some personal Pilates training (lunacy). Then she's back to take care of Dad's

phones, mail, and e-mail, organizing it all and priori-
tizing it for him in neat little color-coded folders with
corresponding sticky tabs (sheer madness).

So you can see how my moping would not be
the most productive contribution to the high-energy
atmosphere.

It's not only the letdown of the carnival that has me
bummed. It's more like that's a catalyst, dragging
me back to the place I was at a few weeks ago when
Logan and I first broke up, when Shelby and Zoë
started pulling away, and when I began to think about
trading in popularity for . . . well, the popular vote.

Which, assuming I still have a shot at that, anyway,
is definitely a shot of the longer variety.

My own campaign isn't over yet, but it sure feels
like my old life is.

I offer to help my mom out, take a position with her
alongside my father's high-speed connection.

"I can file with the best of them," I tell her, feeling
tentative.

And with good reason. She makes a fist and seals
an envelope with the flat of her clenched hand. "Don't
worry. We're fine," she says, effectively dismissing me.

Of course. The truth is, she has it under control.
More than under control.

A good politician knows that even when you're

feeling down and out, you really can't cry uncle before the fat lady sings (a good politician also never met a mixed metaphor that he or she didn't utterly heart). But I kind of do. I cry uncle, aunt, sister, stepmother, and third cousin twice removed.

"Um, well . . . just let me know if you change your mind," I offer lamely, feeling like a stranger in my own house.

I retreat to my bedroom with the *Twist* magazine holiday makeup guide. Historically, my moods are nothing a little swipe of glitter eye pencil can't cure.

But then the strangest thing happens. Like, I literally have to wonder if those buzzings from the fax machine somehow messed with my brain waves, leaving me a hollowed-out shell, a pod-person version of the cool, calm, collected former First Daughter — and Girlfriend — of Plainsboro, Illinois.

Not even *Twist* can help me now.

I try, really I do. I flip through the magazine and gaze longingly at the rich, sumptuous holiday patterns. I allow my eyes to linger on the luxe cocktail dresses and glittering "statement" jewelry that scream "Town Hall New Year's Gala."

And I feel nothing.

Well, not *nothing* exactly. I feel slightly thirsty, and after a minute or two, I feel that my hands are kind of dry. But it's nothing a little moisturizer wouldn't cure. My mind doesn't even flit, not remotely, to the notion of a paraffin manicure or heated hand mitts. Nope, all it wants is regular old Jergen's.

I am over it. Over it all. If I can't save Everett Field, I sure as shish kebab can't be bothered to try to save my cuticles.

I wonder briefly what effect this attitude adjustment will have on my popularity, or current relative lack thereof.

And then I realize: I'm over that, too.

☆ ☆ ☆ ☆ ☆

"You're not being fair."

"Excuse me?" Mom looks up from her stamp-licking duties and regards me dubiously. Sunlight streams in from the picture window, lighting her face and making her sharp, perfect cheekbones even more pronounced.

"You. You're not being fair. You expect me to just blindly support Dad — and Logan — and not have any opinions of my own."

I fold my arms and bear down at her, working the angle that I've got of being the one of us who is standing.

She sighs. "You can have your opinions, Erin," she says. "But it doesn't look good for anyone if you spout off against your father or your boyfriend in public. Your father and I are just asking for a little discretion."

"No," I insist. "You're asking for a gag order. And it's enough already. Unless I'm writing about makeup, movies, or the mall, no one wants to hear it. Well, too bad."

"Erin, *you're* not being fair."

"Fair? What's not fair is you treating me like your own personal Campaign Barbie! You're so concerned with image that you're not interested in how I'm feeling! Admit it — you think I should never have broken up with Logan."

"And you're happy about it?"

"Of course I'm not happy about it! But unlike you, I can't go around pretending that things are picture-perfect when they're not." My voice grows louder. I'm frustrated by the situation with Caswell, with Logan, with my mother . . . with everything. Just . . . everything.

Now I have her attention. "Erin, I won't have you taking that tone with me."

It's the first time in all my sixteen years that I've taken "a tone" with her.

"Buy a dog, Mom," I snap. "They're much more obedient. And they look great in campaign photo shoots."

She's absolutely furious. I can tell because her neck grows redder and redder. But I don't wait to see what she's going to say next.

Instead, I storm from the room.

☆ ☆ ☆ ☆ ☆

I decide that I've been spending too much time in my own head. It's not healthy, if only because lately my own head is kind of a downer. I log onto MySpace only to find that Allie Soren has been posting photos of herself, Shelby, and Zoë working on campaign stuff with Logan. I can't decide if that makes me angry, sad, nostalgic, or some complicated mixture of the three together.

Normally when I'm feeling complicated mixtures, I call Shelby. Or Zoë. Or Logan.

I decide to call Theo. I need social contact, and school doesn't count. I've been studiously avoiding any one-on-one with him ever since our post-movie weirdness, but things are getting sort of desperate. I cave. Maybe Paige is around, anyway. Three's a crowd, right?

"Erin!" Theo says, answering on the first ring.

"You sound way too perky." I want to be suspicious, but then I remember that I was once a perky person, too. "What are you doing?"

"Reading," he says. "Comic books. Nonrequired."

"I approve. I was trying to get into a reading thing myself, magazines and stuff. It didn't work out."

He laughs. "Oh, no. Now what?"

"Now, fun?" I up-talk, turning it into more of a question than a statement.

"Are you asking me or telling me?" He calls me out.

"Fun," I say, more decisive this time. "Definitely."

"How about a movie?" Theo asks.

I pause. Movies are definitely fun, yeah, in an all-encompassing sort of way that is especially appealing to me right now. But. Movies are also where Theo has been known to wander dangerously close to the kissing zone. Eek.

What to do?

"What were you thinking of seeing?" I ask. Maybe he'll suggest a slasher, something gory and gross and completely unromantic.

He names a popular romantic comedy starring someone decidedly perky. Hmm.

168

I'm starting to rethink this course of action, but it may be that I've come too far.

"When?" I ask, hedging, and hoping to buy time.

"Tomorrow night?" he suggests.

And all at once, there it is. My out. It's a good one, too. "It's the election!"

"Not until next week, Erin," Theo says. "And I thought the whole point of a movie was to take your mind off of . . . things," he finishes diplomatically.

"No, the *other* election," I say. "My dad's. It's tomorrow. It's televised." By all my old friends at Channel Three, in point of fact. "There's food and everything."

"Burned coffee?"

"Of course."

"Well then, count me in. I can keep you busy while your mom and dad go into meltdown mode."

I didn't exactly issue an invite, but then again, a second ago I was jonesing for company. And things are still way weird with Mom. A friendy, buffery type could be a good thing.

"Great!" I cover. "Think Paige would want to come?"

"She babysits Tuesday nights," he explains. "So it's just you and me."

"Perfect," I say, a confusing mess of feelings pressing

169

themselves into a heavy lump deep down in my stomach. Well, if nothing else, election night is not exactly sexy, right?

Except for my father's last election. When Logan was there at my side.

"Great," Theo says, completely unaware of the personality disorder that has recently taken me over. "Then it's a date."

Yup. Perfect. Just perfect.

☆ ☆ ☆ ☆ ☆

As I'd figured, Bright Campaign Headquarters — aka the Ramada Inn rte 17 suite 305 — on election night is literally the least sexually charged, flirtatious, pheromone-laden environment that two nonromantically involved teenagers could possibly find themselves in.

There's stale coffee, as Theo predicted, and also a long table of picked-over wraps and sandwiches that I suspect have seen better days. There are laptops and power cords snaking everywhere, and three separate flat-screen TVs, and cell phone chargers everywhere.

I thought I knew chaos, but evidently, I was wrong. This is a previously uncharted level of chaos. This is pandemonium. Even my mom thinks so. She's abandoned her Wife of the Year platform and now stands off to one corner of the room, gnawing away at a thumbnail.

She's ignoring me. It's awkward.

My father's gaze is fixed on the televisions, where Alisha Owens pores thoughtfully over computer print-outs and clutches at a wireless microphone. She's sequestered in a makeshift town hall studio some-where, which seems like it must be cozy. It has to be less stressful than the room we're in right here. We're one big collective live wire.

"Zucker looks like he's barely hanging in," Theo says, sidling up to me.

I nearly jump, he so takes me by surprise. Sidling is no good. Sidling can lead to brushing up, which can segue into leaning. From leaning it's only a short jump to canoodling, which, though vague, is decidedly romantic.

But yes, Zucker. Also known as my father's competition. I can see via flat screen that he's also, so to speak, the only man in the room who's chewed off more of his own fingernails than my mother.

I know just how he feels. Especially since he's probably going to lose.

"He's not going to win this, is he?" Theo asks. I glance at my watch, taking in the second hand as it sweeps across the broad white face of the clock. It's 11:50 (obviously I have no curfew on election night. All sorts of typical rules go out the window on election night). In ten minutes the votes will be tallied. In ten minutes we'll know whether or not Caleb Bright will be serving another term.

I should be tense. But I'm not. It's a no-brainer. And besides, there's more than enough anxiety crackling through the air as it is.

"Erin, any sound bite for the readers of the *Ledger*? How does it feel to be the daughter of Plainsboro's past and possibly future mayor?"

A thin, wan-looking man who definitely needs a good night's sleep sticks a microphone under my nose.

I'm momentarily rendered speechless. This is pretty unusual for me. "G-good," I stutter finally. "I mean, I'm excited for my father."

"Even though his campaign is being funded by the Caswell Corporation? Which is working to rebuild over Everett Field?"

I have no response to this.

Theo links his arm through mine, reading my thoughts again. He smiles at the reporter gently but firmly. "We've got eight minutes to get some fresh air before things go nuts again."

And then he leads us outside.

☆ ☆ ☆ ☆ ☆

It seems like Theo and I have all of our awkward moments (well, two and counting) in deserted parking lots. It's becoming a trend (I mean, two is a trend, right?). He was right, at least, about the fresh air being good for me — but he was wrong about us having a cool eight minutes before things went all crazy.

Way wrong.

Because suddenly, Theo is completely and undeniably leaning in for some full-frontal kissing.

This time, there's nothing hesitant about his effort. Nope. Old Theo dives in with the fervor and determination of a heat-seeking missile. His eyes are semiclosed and his lips — *ew* — are twitching. He's a cute guy, but it must be said — this is not the best look for him.

I'm momentarily stunned, and then it dawns on me that I do still have the power to dodge this advance. I bend deeply to the left like I've just invented a new yoga pose and I'm working my range of flexibility to its utmost.

I hazard a peek at Theo. His puckered lips peck fruitlessly at thin air. He opens his eyes all the way, looking confused.

"Two strikes, huh?" he asks ruefully.

173

I shrug. "Sorry." I narrow my eyes at him. "But . . . I mean — it's weird, right? What with how you're Logan's best friend?"

"More like ex-best friend," he corrects me, then frowns. "That's kind of girlie. Whatever, the point is, we're not that tight ever since I joined your campaign."

"Right."

"Are you honestly telling me that you don't feel *anything* for me?" Theo asks with a half-smile.

I shrug again. I don't know if it's the savviest political tactic, per se, but sometimes honesty really is the best policy. "I don't. I mean, it's not like . . . you know — I mean, you're cute —"

"Don't," he says, mercifully cutting me off. "I get it."

"Maybe I just need a boy break right now," I offer, sending waves of platonicness in his direction. "If I win the election, I can concentrate on student council. And if I don't win, I can slide into an abyss of self-analysis and despair."

"That sounds fun," he says.

"Right?"

He sighs. "Maybe you should hold off on the pit of despair. And in the meantime . . ." He allows his voice to trail off meaningfully.

"Theo!" I swat at him playfully. Now that the honesty ice has been shattered, I feel more comfortable with the playful approach. "I told you. Boy break."

"No, sure, boy break, of course. That's not really where I was going." He clears his throat, suddenly sounding really purposeful. "In the meantime . . . assuming your father wins, of course —"

"Of course —"

"— do you think he might be interested in letting me intern in his office?"

"Well, I guess so," I begin, thinking it over. "He usually takes on at least one high school volunteer per semester. But you might have to get it cleared through the school counselor's off —" I stop abruptly as a thought occurs to me.

Wait a minute. His sudden interest in my campaign. His familiarity with my father.

"Theo. Did you decide to support me so that you could get in with my father?"

He doesn't say anything, but his expression is pretty much the only answer that I need. Then I remember all the times he spent at my house poring over newspaper clippings and photos of my father.

Ew.

"Theo!" My eyes widen. No wonder Logan wrote

him off. What a jerk. This makes his kissy-face sneak attack even grosser.

"Relax, Erin," he says, reaching for me. I shrink away. The time for any affection has definitely passed. "I do believe in you."

Ugh. I'm going to have to take six showers to get his slime off of me.

"What are you going to do if we win?" I demand.

"Work with you, of course," he says. "And maybe even have another chance to get to know your dad."

I know politics is all about networking and working connections, but I still think Theo's whole subterfuge was pretty sleazy. I need *seven* showers. Or maybe I just need to run through a car wash fully clothed.

"Whatever," I say finally.

When I really think about it, Theo is just the latest in a succession of boys in politics who've let me down: Logan, of course, who totally challenged my principles, and my father, who is aligned with my public enemy number one. And now Theo, who may be more into my father's campaign than mine.

I guess, then, that there's not much left to do but to figure out where both of those campaigns are headed, respectively.

I turn back to Theo, hands on my hips. "I'm sure our eight minutes are up."

☆ ☆ ☆ ☆ ☆

Back in the makeshift green "area" of the hotel suite, the mood has shifted considerably. There's a definite sense of triumph. But whose?

It only takes a moment for my eyes to find my mother's, and in that instant, I know. Her cheeks are flushed and her eyes are shining. She grabs me into a bear hug that's warm and comforting, even though I can still feel the ripple of her abs beneath her ribbed sweater coat.

Everything we've been through over the last few months, all of the misunderstandings, the miscommunications, the confrontations. Right now, they don't matter. I feel a surge of warmth, pride, and happiness.

"He did it, Erin!" she shrieks, giddy like a high school girl. "Your father won!"

177

http://firstgirlbright.blogorama.com
November 4, 1:29 am

More on the whole good news, bad news thing.

Specifically? My father won. Which means, really, that Caswell won, too.

Think it over. You can decide for yourself which news is the good stuff. I'll be over here with the spring forecast issue of *Twist.*

Comments (0)

☆ Chapter Thirteen

We're on the front page of the *Ledger*. The morning after the election, the first thing I see is my own face, beaming out proudly from between my parents, who wear expressions of equal joy.

Believe it or not, my father winning the Plainsboro Township mayoral election doesn't have a huge impact on my life. I mean, it was what we'd been hoping for, of course, but it's also what we're accustomed to. More Ted and Mena, more personal assistants, more photo shoots involving judiciously applied antifrizz serum. More Channel Three.

The night of the election, Alisha Owens was super-interested in my reaction to my father's win. Like, does this put more pressure on me to follow in his footsteps and blah-bitty-blah-da-da. Which it does. But with the PHS student council election only three days away, I didn't want to dwell on that whole thing, for fear that my head might actually explode — and there's really no serum in the world for that.

My mother must notice that I am rapidly unraveling — like a cashmere sweater with a pulled thread — because she approaches me after school one afternoon and gently suggests that we "blow off some steam."

I'm skeptical. We really haven't talked since my nervous breakdown of the other afternoon.

"You're not mad at me?" I ask quietly.

"I wasn't thrilled by your behavior the other day, Erin, but I have done some thinking. You did make some good points. And I don't think that I give you enough credit for being so poised and polished whenever your father is in the public eye."

I want to cry. This is the nicest thing that anyone has said to me in days. "I'm in." Of course I'm in.

"Perfect," she says, smiling. "You can borrow a pair of my yoga pants."

Once I realize her angle, I want to protest. But I realize, anyway, that she's right — I need something. Picking at my own split ends is no kind of stress-relief therapy.

I get over the initial trauma of discovering that squeezing into my mother's gym clothes is not exactly an effortless endeavor and huff my way through a power Vinyasa session with her. And even though I want to yak when she takes a spot right up at the front of the class, making the mirror almost her own personal spotlight, I have to admit that there's something to the whole series of contortions we enact over the course of the ninety-minute session. Flipping yourself into an inverted knot may look easy, but I assure you, it's not. Upward dogs, downward dogs, cobras, monkeys . . . it's less like exercise and more like a very meditative trip to the zoo.

"Feeling any better?" Mom asks as we make our way home, sipping iced lattes.

I nod. And I am, honestly, which surprises no one more than myself. Though of course I care about being healthy and in shape and all that, I have long suspected that I'm allergic to exercise. There never seemed to be any other explanation for the fact that I broke out in hives whenever Shelby or Zoë so much as mentioned the gym.

"I feel like a rubber band that's all stretched out," I say, relishing the sensation of every ounce of tension being wrung from my muscles.

"That's yoga," Mom agrees. "That's why I like to start my day with exercise."

"Oh, hey now," I argue, taking another healthy sip at my drink. "All I said was that I'm feeling better. I cop to nothing other than finding yoga to be less horrible

181

than the absolute worst thing in the world. That hardly means I'm ready to adopt it into my daily routine. I don't need any new patterns, thank you very much." I sip my latte as defiantly as I can to show that I mean business.

My mother laughs, then quiets as we pull into our driveway. "What about your old patterns, then, Erin?" she asks softly, seeming to notice something.

"Huh?" I look up, follow her gaze through the windshield and over, having no idea what to expect.

It's Logan. Standing by our house. And he looks like he wants to talk.

☆ ☆ ☆ ☆ ☆

Having Logan in my room is weird. Or rather, it's weird in that it's *not* all that bizarre, because of how, obviously, he's been here a million times before. If I had a dollar for every time I've seen Logan crashed out on my bed, making nice with Olivio, my stuffed gopher (treasured childhood companion, please don't ask or judge), well . . . I could probably save Everett Field on my own personal bankroll.

"So," he says awkwardly, staring at his sneaker-clad feet like they just might be on fire.

182

"Yeah," I say, not sure just what it is that I'm agreeing with. "You're . . . here." That's me, great at seeing what's right out there in plain sight. Where's that class and poise that Alisha Owens was going on about? "With the . . . hereness of you and all."

He flushes, which I have to admit is kind of nice. It's a relief to see that this is uncomfortable for him, too. Though I suppose the lack of eye contact should have been my first giveaway.

"I heard about your dad," he says unnecessarily, since the smallness of our town means that *of course* he heard about my dad. He pauses. "Is Theo interning for him?"

I roll my eyes. "He asked me to pass along a résumé, but Dad wasn't very impressed. By, uh, Theo's *strategies*, you know?"

"Right." Now Logan looks like he wishes his feet really were on fire.

"Wait — you knew he was using me to get to my father?" I ask suddenly, feeling queasy.

He shrugs. "I suspected. But things were so messed up between us . . ." He sighs. "I'm sorry."

He might be on to something with the hoping-for-sudden-disaster thing. If nothing else, it would be a distraction, since we can't seem to look each other in

183

the eyes. We're mainly directing our conversation through Olivio. Pathetic.

"Are things normal with you two?" I ask, my frank curiosity overcoming any codes of social etiquette.

"Whatever," he says, shrugging it off. "You know guys."

"Apparently I don't," I remind him. Considering the total unpredictability of the two I've been dealing with for the last few months or so.

Now Logan actually chuckles, an out-loud hybrid snort-laugh thing that causes him to wipe self-consciously around the corners of his mouth. "Are things normal with *you* guys?"

I shake my head. "I'm a little grossed out, but whatever. It'll be fine." And then, all at once, I'm somehow compelled —"You know that I had no idea, about any of it —"

"Don't sweat it," Logan says, waving one hand casually. "I kind of had a feeling. But it's no big. What's done is done."

"That is a true fact," I say, arranging myself into a cross-legged position at my desk, even though it means I have about thirteen minutes before my right foot falls asleep. My chair faces Logan's. I rest my elbows on my calves, and my chin in my palms.

Logan looks tired. I mean, adorable — Logan always looks adorable, and even exhausted, that dimple is always on the verge of jumping right out at you — but there are shadows underneath his eyes that highlight how bloodshot the eyes themselves are.

I'm a little bit surprised to find that this bothers me. That I don't like thinking of Logan stressed out, tossing and turning and otherwise freaking.

"Speaking of things that are done," I continue slowly, pointedly, "what are you doing here, Logan?"

He sighs and hitches the edges of his hooded sweatshirt around him so that he's more fully engulfed. It's classic Logan, and part of me wants to jump into his lap and pull the sweatshirt around both of us and stay like that for at least an hour or seven.

Kind of a large part of me, if I'm totally, one thousand and fifty percent honest with myself. A very large part of me — possibly the largest part of me possible — really wouldn't mind that one bit.

"I wanted to congratulate you."

I raise an eyebrow skeptically. "For my father's win?" Since he sure isn't congratulating me for *my* win. At least not yet.

"Well, yeah." He looks sheepish. Humble. Two looks that I know for a fact are unfamiliar to him. This is interesting. "And —" He leans over the edge of the chair and down toward his backpack that rests on the floor. He rummages in the bag for a beat or two, then pops back up, proudly brandishing a set of slightly crumpled pages that are stapled together. "I wanted to give you this."

I untwist myself and venture over from my desk to the rocking chair, taking the papers that Logan proffers. I look at them; they're a jumble of smeared signatures in a rainbow of handwritings and inks.

"Names?" I ask, puzzled.

"*Everyone's* names," he confirms. "Well, almost everyone. The phys ed department abstained. Said they didn't think it was appropriate for them to get involved in school politics."

I'm still confused. "You have everyone's names except for the phys ed department?" For some reason, this new information doesn't do a whole lot to illuminate things.

He stands, takes my hands gently in his own. "It's a petition, Erin," he clarifies. "Protesting the sale of Everett Field. I've been circulating it around the school for a week now. Keeping it a secret from you was no easy feat. At least, I always thought you were totally on top of, like, everything." He manages a wry grin.

"Yeah, well, these days, no one's really rushing to

me with the latest gossip," I remind him. "In fact, I think these days, I *am* the latest gossip."

He acknowledges the truth of this statement by taking a deep breath. "Yeah, um . . . some of that is probably my fault."

I stay silent, waiting to see what's coming next.

"Anyway," he goes on, still looking at anything in the room other than my actual face, "I'm going to hand-deliver it to the school board first thing tomorrow morning."

"The petition," I repeat slowly. "You're going to hand-deliver the petition."

He looks at me like I've just spoken Mandarin. "Yes, the petition."

"Why?" I blurt suddenly. It's not really what I mean to say, exactly, but it's the word that comes to mind. *Why did you do this for me? Why did you try to keep it a surprise?*

Why, really, did we break up after all?

"Because," he says, his tone all "duh."

He steps forward.

And kisses me.

It's light, lighter than a passing splash of sunshine as a storm cloud rolls away, but it's a kiss. A bona fide kiss, right on the lips, even though it lasts all of six seconds, with not an instant of lingering.

My eyes pop open, wider than dinner plates.

"Oh," I say. "That."

He nods. "That. Well, a lot of 'thats,' really. I feel dumb about our fight that day. I was a jerk."

"That is another true fact." It really can't be denied. My insides may be bursting in every direction right now, but I can't let him off the hook completely.

"I think most of it had to do with how you were right?" he up-talks. And Logan *hates* up-talking.

"Come again?" I say, patting at the side of my head like I'm trying to coax ocean water out of my ear.

"Give me a break, Erin," he replies, but he's grinning. "You were right. You know it. Even putting aside how much Everett Field means to you —"

The fact that he knows how much the field means to me is thrilling and crushing all at once. It means that the stakes were always just that much higher, his jerkitude that much jerkier.

Concentrate, Erin, I tell myself. *He's trying to apologize.*

" — even without that, I mean, the field means so much. To everyone. And if it doesn't, it should. It's a part of history. *Our* history, here in Plainsboro. Not to mention, do we really need another gas station right in the middle of town?"

I nod. "We do not need more pollutants – or eyesores."

"Which is why I am telling you: You were right."

We look at each other, steadily, and I feel that spark.

"I have to warn you," Logan says, breaking the spell. "I have no idea what the school board will say or do. For all I know, they'll tell me to shove it. I mean, they're not dictated by the student body. So ultimately, it's their choice."

"I understand," I say.

And I do. I understand that Logan is trying, honestly trying. And that his effort involves a major-extra-mega-super-grand gesture of the highest magnitude. He did this for *me*. He gets me, he cares about me, and he wants to make me happy. My ex-boyfriend totally has my back.

My *ex*-boyfriend. Yeah. I'm not wild about that word. Is it too late to rewrite the end of our story?

I have to ask. I'd be lying to myself if I pretended that seeing Logan here now isn't causing a parade of elephants to stampede through my upper chestal region. He was – is – my first love. He has an effect on me. I meant it when I broke up with him, yeah . . . but that doesn't mean I'm over him or anything. Not one little tiny bit. And those elephants aren't over him, either.

"Logan," I begin, feeling shyer than I have since I got my braces taken off back in the sixth grade, "is there any chance —"

The words aren't even out of my mouth before he jumps in. "Definitely," he says, his eyes bright with meaning. "That is, if you think —"

"I think," I assure him. "Though maybe we want to give ourselves a little time, kind of ease back into being in each other's lives." Inspiration hits with all the subtlety of a cinder block. "I know!" The corners of my mouth twitch upward into a devilish grin. "Loser takes the new class president on a pizza picnic at the infamous field of dreams and shattered relationships."

Logan smirks. Even with him smirking, it takes all of my concentration not to fling my arms around him like we're in a romantic comedy. No wonder I've been so miserable the last few weeks. I'm a Logan addict, and I've been in withdrawal, big-time.

"Very sweet," Logan says. "Except for one thing: I'm dropping out of the race."

The very first elephant in my stomach conga line stops short, causing the rest of them to career into the tips of my rib cage. "What are you talking about?"

"Just that," he replies simply. "Come on, Erin. The school is ready for a change. You're it. You deserve it. You care about our school and the students in it. You want what's best for us. How can I compete with that?"

"Are you kidding?" I retort, eyes flashing. "You'd *better* compete with that!" I glare at him teasingly. "Logan," I say slowly, carefully, and with great deliberation, "it's not a true victory until I have kicked your butt from Plainsboro to sometime next century."

His eyebrows dart upward, and his mouth forms a perfect "O" of surprise. Then he shakes his head, laughing.

"All right, then," he says. "You asked for it. We'll wait, see how things play out. Elections are Friday. Friday night, dinner's on you."

I make a *tsk* sound, but I'm smiling. "Logan," I say, "never underestimate the power of the people."

I sneak another glance at the crumpled petition in my hand. Someone's green pen has begun to leak onto the fingertips of my left hand. I know from past experience that it takes major scrubbing action to de-green human fingertips, but still, I truly couldn't care less. Green fingers are a small price to pay for the power of the people.

So many people. And they all signed their name to my cause. They're backing *me*.

Maybe the popular vote isn't the long shot I thought it might be. Stranger things have happened, after all.

Some of them just in the last eight hours.

.

☆ Chapter Fourteen

When Alisha Owens informed me, on the night of my father's election as town mayor, that she planned to attend the Plainsboro High School student body government elections, I must admit, I kind of thought she was kidding.

Apparently, I thought wrong.

I arrive at school on Friday morning to discover that, as if the election itself wasn't stressful enough, I've got my own personal entourage eagerly awaiting my close-up. Plainsboro High may not have a green room, but that doesn't bother Alisha. She's brought her own fully stocked trailer along with her.

Ms. Donatello pounces on me first period. I'm mesmerized by her lustrous red lipstick.

"You're excused from class. Well, technically," she says, brushing her bangs out of her heavily lined eyes, "you're excused from all of the classes. You're supposed to report to the, um, trailer outside. Actually, since I'm student council advisor, so am I."

She looks pretty confused. I would be, too, if I weren't an old pro at all of this by now. I give her a quick, respectful once-over, and run my fingers through the tips of her hair so that they flip under, toward her chin.

"You're perfect," I say. "Let's go."

☆ ☆ ☆ ☆ ☆

Inside the trailer, it's all about sound bites.

Alisha leans toward me, all metallic baby-blue eye-liner and chiclet-white teeth. Without my father around, she's a little more Elizabeth Hasselbeck than Barbara Walters, it seems.

"Would you say that Ms. Donato is like a mentor to you?" She flutters her false eyelashes and attempts to look very serious. I want to point out that she might be more successful if she weren't wearing an off-the-shoulder top in screaming fuchsia.

"Donatello. Yes, completely," I say, not missing a beat.

"No," she corrects me. "I mean, will you say it? Like, now?" Alisha is being kind of hard-core, in an *E! Entertainment News* sort of way.

194

"Ms. Donatello has always been a mentor to me," I parrot with as much emotion as I can muster. At this point, I feel like an automaton. If only. Automatons probably don't need that much sleep.

Logan and I talked last night, over IM. *Good luck,* he told me, adding a classic smiley emoticon after the fact. *You're going to need it.*

I do enjoy that boy's confidence.

Actually, right now I could use a dose of it myself. Normally, an extra squirt of Juicy Couture perfume is all it takes to give me an emotional boost, but for some reason, today? Smelling like a freshly crusted crème brûlée isn't quite doing the trick.

"You look great, Erin," Alisha tells me, like she's perched right inside of my brain, scanning my thoughts in real time as they occur to me.

"Thanks," I say.

Unfortunately, I don't think just looking great is going to do the trick. If it were only about looking great, well ... Logan looks pretty great himself. Trust me on this. I saw him this morning by his locker and he's wearing a tie, and he's tamed his curls with some styling wax that I gave him last year for Christmas, and he looks like a kid on picture day, except twelve times hotter. So looking great might not be enough, in this case. I have to bring the goods.

If the petition is any indication, then people are on my side. Or at least, they're sympathetic to my cause. But the truth is that it was Logan who circulated those lists. For all I know, when people were scribbling their names down, they were effectively casting their lot in with him, not me. There's no way to know.

That is, *until* we know. Which should be in about twenty-seven minutes.

"How does it feel, Erin, knowing that in twenty-six minutes —"

Crap. Twenty-*six*. Ugh. I might have to throw up. What if I have to throw up? Do student council presidents sometimes throw up? At school? While in the process of actively looking great and waiting on election results?

"— you may be on your way to following in your father's footsteps?"

I thought we already covered this, Alisha. It feels like I might throw up. Any minute now. You might want to step back, even. Just a scooch or two.

But of course, that's not the party line answer. So instead, I clasp my hands demurely in my lap, swallow the wave of nausea that threatens to overtake me, and look Alisha right smack in the eye.

"Don't you think," I begin, the very picture, in

my mind's eye, of poise and confidence, "that I already am?"

She laughs, a throaty, tinkling laugh that suggests that I am the undiscovered comic voice of my generation, laying a hand delicately on my tweed-clad knee.

"So true, Erin," she says, beaming like she's Julia Roberts at the Oscars. "So true." Suddenly I really do feel like my father's daughter.

☆ ☆ ☆ ☆ ☆

Shelby and Zoë come crashing through the curtain that divides the backstage area from the rest of the high school auditorium, and that's how I know.

I've won.

Ballots are cast online, and it's up to Ms. Donatello to run the tallies. I don't envy her. Emotions have been running pretty high in the halls all day long.

For the past hour and a half, while she goes over the computer reports, Logan and I have been sitting on plastic chairs in this makeshift backstage holding pen like we're castoffs from the latest reality television craze. If only. That would be slightly less pressure than the current situation.

That is, until Zoë comes streaking toward me full throttle, shrieking in a frequency I suspect is best heard by members of the canine species. Shelby follows behind at a slightly more dignified pace.

"Congraaaaaats!" she says, drawing the word out as dramatically as possible. Sparkling. The girl is sparkling. Maybe she wrangled her way into Alisha Owens's trailer when I wasn't looking, got her hands on the body glitter.

Does she not remember, like, how she didn't talk to me for a month? I mean, really.

For a moment, I'm dumbfounded. "Did I —"

"Of *course*," Z says, giggling madly.

And I realize — that's it. The girl is mad. All this time, it was so simple.

And you know what? I need less madness in my life, I decide. I've got enough going on as it is.

Especially if I'm Plainsboro High's new STUDENT COUNCIL PRESIDENT!

Logan catches my eye, squeezes my hand, and then ushers me through the curtain — right past Zoë and Shelby. We move toward the crowd.

As you might have expected, it's a throng. Again.

But this time, I'm ready for it.

☆ ☆ ☆ ☆ ☆

I step forward toward the podium, squinting slightly at the bright fluorescent lights of the auditorium. My arms are grabbed on either side of me by shapeless bodies — it's all a huge blur — and I'm steadied.

All at once, I totally get it.

I can see why my father and Logan both are so addicted to the public eye. I mean, yeah, there's the whole noble aspect of it, the lobbying-for-change thing, but also? Standing here, in front of a room of a few hundred people who are cheering for me? Who voted for me? Who want (for the most part, that is), *me*?

It's a rush.

I'm feeling light-headed, and I momentarily wish I'd been able to force down more than just an apple this morning. Then again, I'm not sure my blood sugar is really the reason I'm suddenly seeing the room in a complicated system of double images.

I shake it off.

I smooth my hair down at my shoulders, quickly adjust the hem of my skirt, and lean into the microphone, resting my French-manicured hands on either side of the podium.

"I did have a little speech prepared," I say, because I did. "But I think I might have left it in my locker. I promise, though, that I'm really not the flighty or forgetful type."

A murmur of laughter. They're on my side. They voted for me! Majority rules.

"I have a confession to make," I say, giving the room a moment to fall silent again. "I wasn't so sure about running for student council.

"You guys know me, and you know that politics has always been for the guys in my life. My job has been to make them look good — not that it's always easy!

"Logan Tanner learned the hard way that all I really needed was a cause to rally for, and after that, there'd be no holding me back. He didn't make it easy — and I'm grateful to him for that. I take personal credit for converting him to a place of eco-consciousness and better living through petitioning.

"Logan told me that what the school needs is change.

"But it doesn't matter, really, what Logan thinks. It matters what *you* think. The vote is — was — in *your* hands. And I'm honored that you chose me.

"We may have lost the first fight for Everett Field. I wasn't able to win that one for you guys. But it's only the beginning. For us. Together.

"We're going to have an amazing year."

The room breaks out into noisy shrieks and hollers, foot-stomping and clapping and even a rogue wave or two popping up along the periphery of the neat rows of folding chairs. I'm exhausted, but I'm exhilarated. I did it. I won.

I may have lost Everett Field, but I won the election. And I'm going to keep fighting and, hopefully, win a whole lot more, too.

☆ ☆ ☆ ☆ ☆

As I step away from the podium, smiling in what I hope is a modest but confident manner, a palm cups my hip. I turn. It's Theo.

"We did it." He grins. "You did it."

"*We* did it," I admit. He may be sleazier than I thought, and yeah, he definitely has his own agenda, but I owe Theo a lot. If he and Paige hadn't come through for me when they did, I don't know that I would have been able to pull this whole thing off. A person needs friends. A support system.

Theo rolls his eyes. "Whatever. I mean, sure, thanks. But listen . . ." Now he leans in like he's going to hit me with some major gossip, or maybe wipe a stray eyelash off of my cheek or something like that. "What do you say to a victory dinner? Just the two of us?"

The boy has *always* got an angle, and his angles are

brimming with sharp, pointy edges that creep me out. *How* have I not seen this before?

"Right," I say. "Uh, but, I've kind of got plans."

I do. I mean, I think I do. At least, I hope I do.

I really, really hope so.

☆ *Chapter Fifteen*

If you've never been to an inaugural ball, you might think that it sounds sort of stuffy and grown-up. And while you wouldn't be entirely wrong, I must say that oftentimes, those grown-ups know how to get down.

My father's inaugural ball is one of those times.

But I think that in order to fully set the scene for this lavish affair, I should go back even further, explain how, exactly, I wound up here, chin pressed up against the starched, pressed, and impeccably tailored shoulder of a very 007-looking tuxedo — and the cute boy to whom the tuxedo, and the shoulder, belong. . . .

☆ ☆ ☆ ☆ ☆

Those plans I mentioned to Theo earlier involved yet another attempt to surprise Logan, in the hopes that this second take would go more smoothly than my first time around.

This time, I don't bother with the blindfold, because, I mean, *duh*, but when we arrive at Everett Field, I've got the picnic blanket and the candles and all of that fun stuff. It's kind of chilly now, it being November and all, so the candles keep winking out in the crisp late-autumn breeze, but somehow, that doesn't take away from the emotion of the moment.

Logan must feel it, too, because he takes my hand in his own and gives it a squeeze.

Honestly, being back at the field feels wonderful. There's no tension involved, no doubt. We laugh and cuddle together again. Which, after nearly two months of not being able to smile with Logan, to poke him in the ribs when I feel that he is not fully appreciating the magnitude of my comedic talent, or to watch his eyes crinkle up when he lets loose with a gut-busting guffaw . . . well, to laugh with him now feels nice. *Really* nice.

"I thought we were going to get pizza," he says, looking down at the bare checkered blanket. "I owe *you* a pizza."

"I was," I say, "but then I realized that pizza's kind of . . . boring."

"*Boring.*" He arches an eyebrow. "Oh, man. Are you

going to get all high and mighty now that you're a small-town celebrity?"

I make a *pshaw* face.

"I was always a small-town celebrity," I remind him. "Even that brief stint of social pariah-dom was really just par for the course. Me and Britney Spears, you know? It's so typical. But now, it's all about the come-back." I do a little jazz-hands move, just for old times' sake.

He shakes his head, clearly waiting for me to continue, so I decide to let him off the hook and get on with it.

"Anyway . . ." I flip my hair back off of my face as the wind tickles the edges of my cheeks. "We can do better than pizza."

"Better than half double pepperoni, half mushroom and olive?" Logan seems extremely dubious. I don't necessarily blame him. Those black olives are seriously my weakness.

I nod, though, trying to convey authority. "Tonight, we can do better than that. You're going to have to trust me."

And, for the first time in what feels like ages, he agrees to do just that.

☆ ☆ ☆ ☆ ☆

When the doorbell rings, I curse to myself and slip an amethyst cocktail ring onto my finger.

"That's Logan!" I shout. "Can somebody *please* answer the door?"

My mother says she will, and I hear her heels clicking on the hardwood floor. Her voice and Logan's mix together in a murmured jumble. Then my father joins in.

One last squirt of perfume, and I'm ready.

I make my way to the top of the stairs, feeling surprisingly nervous. My skin prickles with anticipation.

I see Logan, and my heart catches in my throat. I pause at the landing.

"Wow."

He's wearing a tuxedo and his hair is still slightly wet from the shower. His eyes sparkle. I want to slide down the banister and into his arms. If only I weren't wearing skintight satin.

"Wow, yourself." Logan's eyes tell me that he'd slide *up* the banister to me if he could.

"Ready to get down, inaugural ball–style?" I ask, stepping carefully down the staircase in my delicate heels.

"We all are." My father beams at me and claps me on the shoulder. "And we're *all* celebrating. This party is for you as well as me."

"Dad, that's so sweet." And so unexpected.

"I'm proud of you, Erin. Even though you had to go head-to-head with me. And so tonight is your night as well as mine. I've opened the party up to your classmates."

My jaw drops. "Did you know about this?" I ask, turning to Logan.

"There was an e-mail invite sent out. But we were told that it was a surprise for you." He leans over and pecks me on the cheek. "Surprise."

☆ ☆ ☆ ☆ ☆

There are definite perks to being small-town royalty. For instance, on the night that your father is being sworn in as town mayor, you might find yourself squeezed into a shimmering lavender gown — seriously, not a dress but an actual *gown*, like you were off to thank the Academy or something — that dips in at the waist and fans back out down and across the floor around you, like an extremely elegant mermaid's tail. You might even note that atop your much-sprayed, beauty-queen, back-combed updo, a tiara that weighs more than an unabridged dictionary shimmers like a beacon. Your teeth might tingle with the after-effects of some extreme Crest Whitestrips action, but you will know that it is all worth it.

You look — and feel — like a princess.

And truly, one of the very best aspects of discovering oneself in a princesslike state is the promise of a real, live Prince Charming.

Have I mentioned that Logan looks *hot* in a tux? He does. Not even remotely penguin-esque.

My parents were thrilled to see Logan and me out on the town doing the bona fide date thing again. They shook his hand and offered him some sparkling water as he settled himself into the stretch limo that was to serve as the evening's transportation. Seeing as how it was my father's night and all, they probably had other stuff on their minds, too.

So, yeah. Those people who think that politicians don't know how to celebrate or to let their hair down? They should come see my dad sometime. Mind you, Caleb Bright keeps his hair closely shorn and quite respectable, but there is nothing dignified about the chickenlike boogie that he's currently engaged in, smack in the center of the dance floor. I know my mother tolerates it because it makes her look good.

"I think you may have inherited his dance moves," Logan says, laughing in my parents' direction.

I narrow my eyes at him. "You're lucky you're cute."

He gazes at me meaningfully. "I'm lucky for a lot of things."

I contemplate swooning, quickly assessing the potential damage to my control-top, body-slimming undergarments. Fortunately, I am saved by the sound of a spoon clinking against a champagne glass, the universal indication that it's time to start the toasting.

The dance floor clears as people shuffle themselves into a half-moon shape around the stage that's been constructed for this evening. People clasp Mardis Gras beads, sequined eye masks, and DVD singles from the karaoke booth outside. My father and his people went all-out. It really is quite the shindig. I make a mental note to pencil in some time for air guitar and *High School Musical* reenactments after the speechifying is over and done with.

My father steps to the microphone, and once again, I'm taken by how sophisticated he looks. If George Clooney (a totally classy old Hollywood actor) had gone into politics, he would have been a lot like my dad, I think.

"I just want to welcome you all here tonight, and to thank you again for coming and for supporting me."

People clap politely. They're excited, but a little more subdued than everyone was at my election. I think that's just the difference between teenagers and grown-ups. Hormones and stuff.

Hence all the hooting and hollering from the peanut gallery in the form of Paige, Theo, and Mindy. Oh — and Ms. D., who is definitely a kid at heart.

"As you know, this is a very special night for me," he goes on, "not just because I'm being sworn in for my second term but also because I am sharing the excitement of sweeping the vote with my daughter, Erin, who has recently gotten into the politics game."

Suddenly, a burst of spotlight rushes toward me, and I feel the room as a whole turn and gape. I'm very, very glad that the tiara is fastened by several pounds of steel hairpins.

"Just last week, Erin was voted president of the Plainsboro High School student council," Dad says, "and I couldn't be prouder of her. Even if she did go head-to-head with the Caswell Corporation, my primary campaign funders."

I think maybe I would like it if the floor opened up and swallowed me in one gulp, but I take a deep breath. Logan catches my gaze and winks, which reassures me.

"Erin, as I told you earlier this evening, I think of tonight as not *my* inaugural ball but *ours*. Will you come up here and join me?"

Will I? Well, as long as that tiara is firmly affixed to my head, I absolutely will. I shimmy up to the stage as quickly as the rather restrictive fabric of my gown will allow. I scramble up next to my father, who squeezes me around the shoulders with all of his might.

"It took a lot of courage for you to go head-to-head with me, and with big business," he says, prompting a long whistle from someone out in the crowd. "And there's someone here who has something else to say about that."

A small, round man in a suit, wearing tiny, wire-rimmed glasses, lumbers up to the stage. My stomach sinks.

"This is Wayne Warner," my father says. "President and CEO of the Caswell Corporation."

I kind of want to hate Wayne Warner, seeing as how he's the embodiment of all evil, and, frankly, my very own archnemesis. But it's hard to hate a man who is currently dabbing at his receding hairline with a worn green cotton handkerchief. And then when he takes the microphone, it's all over for me, for good.

In the best possible way, that is.

"Erin Bright," he begins, his tone booming, "I have in my hands a petition that the school board delivered to me this afternoon."

The petition. Right. With everything that had

happened in the last few days, I completely forgot about that. Yikes.

"It seems that you and most of your classmates are interested in saving Everett Field," he says.

I nod. This isn't exactly news.

"Well"— he clears his throat —"I regret to inform you that, unfortunately, that's not in the cards. And you should know that the gas station we intend to build on the site of the field will boost this town's tax revenue by an estimated twelve percent."

I blink, feeling queasy. Where is he going with this?

"What we at Caswell Corp. cannot do, however, is stand by as construction demolishes the spirit of our town's youth."

This sounds promising. My ears perk up.

"We'll give you three hundred square feet of untouched field, with which you can do whatever you choose. It will be declared a historic site in perpetuity, and you have my personal guarantee that it will never be sold or otherwise threatened."

Three hundred square feet? That's the size of my parents' screened-in patio.

Okay, it's not a football field, but I can *totally* live with that.

"Also"— he coughs —"since you and your classmates

have impressed us with your commitment to the environment, Caswell has pledged that our new gas station will sell eco-friendly biodiesal — *and* we will plant a row of trees on Main Street in your honor."

In your honor.

Who knew?

I've got a dad who supports me, even when I'm not exactly supporting him. I've got a mom who understands the importance of the sound mind/sound body connection, even if she goes a tad overboard with the whole external appearances thing every now and then. I've got a new-old boyfriend who completely gets me, loves me for who I am, and *likes* that I kicked his butt. I've got the student council presidency, and a bench in Everett Field where I can people-watch to my heart's content. I've got *trees*.

And now, apparently, I've got honor, too.

Cool, right?

Logan flashes me a thumbs-up. I blow a tiny, almost imperceptible kiss right back at him. And then I fling my arms around my father with all my might, giving no thought to whether or not the satin of my dress is going to wrinkle.

The cheers are deafening.

Another thing I've got? Something new to write about. It's not *Restless Nature,* but it's mine.

Since my father's election – *and* my own – I've
had a few days to finally stop, breathe, reflect. And
I've come to some realizations.

It seems like I've crafted an entire high school
career out of being popular. And it's a very particular
type of popularity: one that's borne of proximity to
swaggery, good-looking student-leader types, or
the mild celebrity attached to being the mayor's
daughter. It doesn't have a whole lot to do with
anything other than my not-so-unique ability to
straighten my hair flatter than Lauren Conrad's,
and to toe the party line.

But as I've learned, life is way more than a party,
even when it seems like you spend huge, obscene
chunks of time clinking glasses of sparkling water

214

with the supergorgeous Alisha Owenses of the world, or kicking the town treasurer's butt in a call-and-response karaoke version of "Summer Lovin'" from *Grease* (true story). Life is about hard choices and speaking up when you think that something isn't right.

Or, at least, *my* life is. These days, that is.

It's true, I didn't take Caswell Corp. down. It's going to be gas-station-tastic here in a few short months, once construction gets under way. It's going to be loud and annoying, and it's going to interfere with trig class (like I needed another distraction during math?). But I did make myself — and all of us — heard. And that's something. That's something *big*.

That's something even bigger, if possible, than the popular vote.

When I attended my father's inaugural ball (excuse me, I mean, my father's and *my* inaugural ball, as I've been strongly prompted), I felt magical. Like a fairy princess who'd been given her happy ending (and really awesome shoes).

It's not the ending, though, is it? The limo went back at the end of the night, sure, and for all I know, it's morphed back into a pumpkin. But we've got a corner of Everett Field, which I know we'll all cherish. And we've got a promise of greener endeavors yet to come.

We've got a year together, all of us, to keep working, and fighting, and changing things. Changing our own little corner of the world.

And I have it on good authority that we've got Logan Tanner in our corner, too. Mmm . . .

So really, as much as this is my perfect, dreamworld happy ending, even with the seventeen hours it's going to take to remove my Silver Eggplant nail polish, it's just as much a beginning. For all of us. And just as happy, too.

It's a new era, with a whole new party line. And you're all on the guest list.

I do still love a good party.

To Do List: Read all the *Point* books!

By Aimee Friedman
- ❑ South Beach
- ❑ French Kiss
- ❑ Hollywood Hills
- ❑ The Year My Sister Got Lucky

- ❑ **Airhead** by Meg Cabot

- ❑ **Suite Scarlett** by Maureen Johnson

- ❑ **Love in the Corner Pocket** by Marlene Perez

- ❑ **This Book Isn't Fat, It's Fabulous** by Nina Beck

Hotlanta series by Denene Millner and Mitzi Miller
- ❑ Hotlanta
- ❑ If Only You Knew

- ❑ **Top 8** by Katie Finn

- ❑ **Popular Vote** by Micol Ostow

By Pamela Wells
- ❑ The Heartbreakers
- ❑ The Crushes

Summer Boys series by Hailey Abbott
- ❑ Summer Boys
- ❑ Next Summer
- ❑ After Summer
- ❑ Last Summer

- ❑ **Orange Is the New Pink** by Nina Malkin

Making a Splash series by Jade Parker
- ❑ Robyn
- ❑ Caitlin
- ❑ Whitney

In or Out series by Claudia Gabel
❑ In or Out ❑ Loves Me, Loves Me Not
❑ Sweet and Vicious ❑ Friends Close, Enemies Closer

Once Upon a Prom series by Jeanine Le Ny
❑ Dream ❑ Dress ❑ Date

❑ **To Catch a Pirate** by Jade Parker

I ♥ Bikinis series
❑ He's with Me by Tamara Summers
❑ Island Summer by Jeanine Le Ny
❑ What's Hot by Caitlyn Davis

❑ **Kissing Snowflakes** by Abby Sher

By Erin Haft
❑ Pool Boys ❑ Meet Me at the Boardwalk

❑ **Secret Santa** by Sabrina James

Little Secrets series by Emily Blake
❑ 1: Playing with Fire ❑ 2: No Accident
❑ 3: Over the Edge ❑ 4: Life or Death
❑ 5: Nothing but the Truth ❑ 6: Lock and Key

Story Collections
❑ **Fireworks: Four Summer Stories** by Niki Burnham, Erin Haft, Sarah Mlynowski, and Lauren Myracle

❑ **21 Proms** Edited by Daniel Ehrenhaft and David Levithan

❑ **Mistletoe: Four Holiday Stories** by Hailey Abbott, Melissa de la Cruz, Aimee Friedman, and Nina Malkin

www.thisispoint.com